What's the Opposite of a Best Friend?

**Other Apple paperbacks
you will enjoy:**

Boys Are Yucko
by Anna Grossnickle Hines

Eenie, Meanie, Murphy, No!
by Colleen O'Shaughnessy McKenna

The Friendship Pact
by Susan Beth Pfeffer

The Lemonade Trick
by Scott Corbett

Marshmallow Muscles, Banana Brainstorms
by Karen T. Taha

Yours Turly, Shirley
by Ann M. Martin

What's the Opposite of a Best Friend?

A. Bates

AN
APPLE
PAPERBACK

SCHOLASTIC INC.
New York Toronto London Auckland Sydney

To the whole crew —
  Marla, Kim, M-Tom, Danyul & Carol,
Donald, Clinton & Ruth, Cleve & Gaynelle, Court
& Pam, Sheldon & Mistie, Ramona & Vince,
Clifton —
  For years of support, love and enthusiasm.
Thanks!

  And thanks to Judy Ernst for asking Alia to
be a bus buddy in the first place.

ISBN 0-590-44145-0

12 11 10 9 8 7 6 5 4 3 2   1 2 3 4 5 6/9

Printed in the U.S.A.   40

First Scholastic printing, November 1991

Contents

1.
Buddies

"Jenelle, wait up!"

"Hi, Stace," I called. I watched her while I waited for her to catch up with me.

Stacy is pretty. She's small and has really dark hair that makes her skin look very pale. And she has hazel eyes, which I think is exotic.

I mean, my eyes are plain blue. They're not sky-blue, or sapphire, or turquoise. Just blue. And my hair is plain blonde. It is naturally wavy, which is kind of neat, but it's not towhead, strawberry, or honey-blonde. Just blonde. It's okay, I guess. Boring, but okay.

Stacy caught up with me. "Did you get your report done?" she asked.

I nodded. "I did it on team play in football."

Stacy giggled. "I should have known!" she said. "I did mine on why people should keep a diary." She patted the notebook she always carries.

"I wonder if the new boy is here yet," she said as we walked across the playground toward the sixth-grade door.

I made a face at Stacy. "Maybe you should have written your report on boys," I said. "That's all you think about. Anyway, I think Ms. Kennedy made it up. It's been two weeks, and he's not here."

"She wouldn't make it up," Stacy said. "I'm dying for him to get here. The boys in our grade are hopeless."

"The new boy will be in our grade," I pointed out. "Don't get your hopes up, Stace. He'll be hopeless, too. But maybe he'll like to play football," I added.

"Now *you're* the one who's hopeless!" Stacy told me. "It isn't normal for a girl to be so uninterested in boys."

"I like boys," I protested.

"Sure," Stacy agreed. "While they're playing football."

Sometimes I wonder how we got to be such good friends. Stacy is totally, completely boy crazy. And she's right. I only like boys to play football with. I love football. I love playing it, watching it, and talking about it. My only problem is, I love all the teams, so I have trouble deciding whom to cheer for.

I have fourteen different NFL team T-shirts and three team sweatshirts. Stacy has none.

What she does have is fourteen different boys hanging out around her at recess, and at least three more wishing they were brave enough to join the crowd. I have quite a few boys around me, too, but we're playing football.

You could say Stacy and I are opposites.

The new boy wasn't in class that day, either, and Stacy looked glum until Ms. Kennedy made the day's announcements.

Mostly they were the usual things like hamburger deluxe for hot lunch, and we weren't supposed to jump in the puddles out on the softball field.

But she had a different announcement, too.

"The district has given approval for the preschoolers to ride the bus," she told us. "That means there will be three- and four-year-olds riding with you. All the grades are supposed to have a discussion about making the little ones feel welcome."

Ms. Kennedy smiled at us. "You don't need to be told that. You're very good with the preschoolers on the playground. You know they look up to you, and I'm sure you wouldn't pick on a preschooler.

"So we'll get right to the good stuff. The preschool teacher would like each child to have his or her own sixth-grade bus buddy to sit with them on the bus and help them on and off."

Stacy and I looked at each other. I thought it

3

sounded like it might be fun to be a buddy, and I could tell Stacy did, too. The preschoolers only go to school two mornings a week, either Monday and Wednesday, or Tuesday and Thursday. I guess it's kind of unusual to have preschoolers at a regular school, but the district is trying something new. They're always trying something new. At least having preschoolers around is a better experiment than having the school board try out a new math program on us!

"There are only eleven preschoolers who need buddies," Ms. Kennedy said. "If you want to be a buddy you'll need to fill out an application. You can turn it in at the office."

She pointed to the applications on her desk. "Just get one sometime today if you're interested. Now, English reports. Get them out, everyone."

Stacy and I discussed the buddy program at lunch.

"I think it would be kind of neat," Stacy said. "I always wanted a little sister or brother. The preschoolers are really cute." She ate her hard-boiled egg, which her mother packs for her — already peeled — along with a little plastic package of salt and pepper. Then she got out her deli sandwich and the little package of mustard her mother puts in. Stacy says mustard, ketchup, and mayonnaise make the bread soggy if you put them on the sandwich in the morning, so her mom

4

buys little packages and Stacy puts it all on her sandwich at lunch.

"They are cute," I agreed, watching her eat. I took out my peanut butter sandwich, plain, which I'd packed for myself — with no little package of jelly.

Stacy and I are both the only kids in our families, which has good points and bad points. From visiting friends who have brothers and sisters I'd say the bad points are that there's no one else to share the blame, and that an only child doesn't get much practice baby-sitting. The good points are pretty obvious. There's no one else to make noise and bother you and get into your things.

"Let's do it," I said, watching Stacy eat her sliced fruit. I couldn't decide if I was disgusted with Stacy's lunch, or envious. Whichever it was, I should have been used to it! "I'll bet being a bus buddy would count as experience for baby-sitting."

Stacy nodded thoughtfully. "I think my buddy will be a little girl," she said. "All cute and ruffly."

"I hope mine isn't," I said.

After the lunch football game, which I play in and Stacy sometimes watches, we each took an application from Ms. Kennedy's desk. I had mine filled out even before I got on the bus to go home.

The application wanted to know my name, age, grade, and my teacher's name, plus whether I had little brothers or sisters at home, and whether I always rode the bus or only sometimes did.

All that was easy. I'm Jenelle Miller, almost twelve, sixth grade, and my teacher is Ms. Kennedy. I have no little kids at home, and I always ride the bus because both my parents work. If I miss the bus, I have no other way of getting to school.

All I needed was Mom's signature, and that was easy. She thought it was a great idea.

"Check the schedule," Mom reminded me after she'd signed my application. "I made a new one, but I don't remember what you're *On For*."

Mom says life is too hard without a schedule because you're always two steps behind yourself.

Personally, I think life is too hard WITH a schedule. I'd rather just do things when I feel like doing them.

I checked. I was *On For Baking Duty*. I don't mind that job. I made chocolate chip cookies. That way, if I got my bus buddy this week, I'd have something nice to share with her . . . or him.

2.
The New Boy

Tuesday I wore my Vikings T-shirt. As I headed toward the front door of the school to turn in my application, I saw two little boys waving their arms at me.

"Hey, big kid!" one boy called. "He took my ball!" The boy had blond hair kind of sticking up all over his head. Maybe he didn't know how to comb it yet. He was pretty little, but he was still bigger than the other boy.

"Uh-uh!" the other boy denied. "Mine!"

"I had it first!" the bigger boy insisted.

The smaller boy was awfully cute. He had long brown hair, big brown eyes, and rosy cheeks. He looked like a tiny angel.

But I knew I had to be fair. I couldn't give the ball to the smaller boy just because he was cuter.

I squatted, looking the boys in the eye.

7

"It was his ball, wasn't it?" I asked the cute little boy.

He nodded. "But I founded it," he said.

"It wasn't losted," the blond said.

"Then I think it's still his," I said.

The dark-haired angel stuck his tongue out at me, kicked me in the shin, and ran to join the group of preschoolers who were filing off the playground toward their classroom.

"Hooray!" shouted the blond. He grabbed the ball and ran off, too. I scrambled up, trying to ignore the pain in my shin as I joined Stacy in the front hall. We turned in our applications together. Our office receptionist, Mr. Hines, is a football fan, too, but he thinks the Houston Oilers are the only team that matters.

He frowned. "The Vikings are nobody," he told me.

"How many times have they been to the Super Bowl?" I asked.

"How many of those times have they won it?" he asked.

"Even when you lose the Superbowl it still means you're second best in the world," I told him. "What have the Oilers done recently?"

"I can't believe this!" Stacy said. "Football, football! I can't even call you on Sunday or Monday because of the games!"

"You could call at halftime," I said.

"But I'd have to watch part of the game to know

when halftime was," she said. She shivered, as if the idea disgusted her.

I guess it does. Like I said, Stacy doesn't like football at all.

The new boy was in class when we got there.

I could tell that Stacy approved! She stared and smiled, looking suddenly dreamy. If I knew Stacy, she was falling in love again!

I didn't see anything so special. He was pretty tall, taller than I am, and I'm fairly tall. He had a deep voice. A lot of boys in our grade don't yet. He also had curly brown hair and bright blue eyes—sapphire-blue. Not plain blue like mine.

But I wasn't impressed until lunchtime. When I got to the field, the new boy was already there, tossing the Nerf football, which is the only kind we're allowed to use at school. He was tossing it clear across the field to Jason. He threw a beautiful pass!

Now, that's impressive!

I stood there, impressed, watching while he threw pass after pass, waiting for someone to toss the ball to me.

No one did. The guys all kept yelling to the new kid, telling him how great he was, calling for him to toss the ball to them. He was good, I'll admit that. Maybe even as good as I am.

I'm not bragging when I say I can throw. I can lob the ball, arc it, pass between two people and get it right to the one I'm aiming at, and fire it way downfield. I've always been the quarterback, clear back since second grade when we were first learning to play football. And I — the quarterback — had been dumped. I'd been left standing on the sidelines while a new kid took over!

Because he is a boy! I thought. It doesn't matter how good I am, or how long I've been quarterback . . . because I'm a girl. Let a guy come in, and the whole team forgets me.

I couldn't believe it. Four years I'd been playing with those guys and in one afternoon, I was nothing. They didn't even realize I was gone.

Finally I stalked over to sit on the bench, fuming while I watched.

"Isn't he great?" Stacy asked as we walked back into class.

"Oh, yeah, great," I said crossly. She didn't even notice! I thought, still furious. The first time in history there's been a game going and I didn't play, and all she notices is the guy who played in my place! "What's his name?" I asked.

"Mark," she said. "Mark Turner. He's really cute," she added, looking dreamy-eyed.

Adorable, I thought. Absolutely adorable.

3.
Replacement Quarterback

By the next day I was so mad I didn't even try to play football. I stood with the girls all recess. Once one of the guys — Jason — motioned to me to join them, but I just shook my head. I was glad someone had noticed I was missing, but it was going to take more than one guy wanting me back before I started playing again.

Besides, I thought, it might occur to those guys eventually that we could get two teams going since we had two quarterbacks.

But it didn't seem to occur to anyone that there were two quarterbacks. It didn't seem to occur to anyone that they were missing someone important. And I wasn't going to force my way in. That's one thing I've noticed about Stacy. She just assumes everyone wants to do things her way, and I'm not like that. I never will be. I like Stacy, but I'll never be like her!

Friday, when I went over to stand with Stacy again, she quit gushing about Mark long enough to ask me why I wasn't playing.

"The guys have a new quarterback," I said stiffly. I was glad she had finally noticed, but it sure took her long enough!

Stacy looked at Mark again. "Yeah," she said. "I wonder if he's noticed me."

I wonder if you'd notice if I strangled both of you, I thought. Can't you see there's a problem here? I'm not out there playing football! I've been replaced, and all you can do is make eyes at my replacement!

I was hurt, but it's dumb to be angry at Stacy for being blindly interested in a boy. For as long as I've known her, she's been blindly interested in one boy or another, one right after the other. That's Stacy. Still, she could have offered me a little sympathy. We are supposed to be best friends.

"What's the opposite of a best friend?" I muttered, but I guess she didn't hear me.

We didn't hear a word about bus buddies until Friday afternoon. Then everyone who had applied had to go for a short interview.

I was a little nervous waiting my turn because I'd never had an interview before. But Mrs. Benson, the preschool teacher, is very nice, so I wasn't nervous once we got talking.

12

She explained that bus buddies would have a badge to wear until their preschooler knew them, and that we would meet our buddies before they started riding the bus.

"It'll take some of the parents a while to get used to the idea of sending their preschooler on the bus," Mrs. Benson said. "But I'm sure within a week or two we'll need all of our buddies.

"All you really have to do is be on the bus the mornings your buddy rides, and let them sit with you. You need to take responsibility for them during evacuation practice. The district is concerned the little ones will slow everyone down in case of emergency. And some of the kids live across the street from the bus stop. If yours is one of them, you'll need to go across and hold his or her hand until you're seated again."

She smiled, and her eyes sparkled. I could see why the little kids liked her. "It's very important to have a special person nearby when you're only three years old," she said. "Your buddy might be a little nervous the first few days, so be ready with the hugs and hold his or her little hand! That's important!"

I nodded again. "I'd like to be a bus buddy," I said. "It sounds like fun, and it sounds like an important job. And I'm always on the bus."

She smiled. "I think you'd make a good bus buddy, Jenelle. We'll let you know next week."

4.
Girl Stuff

Saturday is our errand day, and Mom took me shopping.

Mom is usually pretty understanding. I can talk to her about almost anything. But today she was being very stubborn.

I needed new socks desperately. I'm very hard on socks, for some reason. It seems like every time I put on a pair, they're thinner than the last time I wore them, and before I know it, they're full of holes.

Mom sighs, and accuses me of chewing them in my sleep, but she gets me new ones.

We didn't have any problem with the socks. She just handed me two packages of the kind I like — white ones, almost knee high, like the football players wear.

But then she handed me a package of panty hose, too, one of those white plastic eggs.

I stared at the egg, read the cardboard piece that fits around the bottom and sides, and finally said, "What's this for? It's not your size."

"It's your size. They're for you."

"I don't want panty hose," I said.

"You need at least one pair," she said, looking determined.

"Why?" I asked. "I can't play football in panty hose."

"Oh, for concerts and stuff like that."

"There won't be any concerts for a long time," I pointed out. "Not until Christmas."

"So you're getting them early," she said. "You know I like being prepared."

That was true. She likes being organized and prepared. But I didn't see why that meant I had to have panty hose.

"You know," I said, sounding thoughtful. "Last year I just wore regular socks to the Christmas concert."

Mom shuddered. "I know," she said. "And sneakers. I nearly died of embarrassment."

"I was comfortable. I didn't mind."

"I did," Mom said firmly.

I guess it's not such a big deal, I thought. If it makes her feel better, I'll let her buy me panty hose. At least it's not dumb tights this year. And there are lots of places an egg can get lost before Christmastime!

"Okay," I agreed.

15

Maybe I should have put up more of a fuss because next she steered me over to the bras and silky underwear.

"Nope!" I said. I shook my head. "I don't want any."

"Now, Jenelle," Mom began.

I knew that tone of voice! She used it on me when I was little and wouldn't take my medicine. She used it when I wouldn't try artichoke hearts.

"This stuff isn't like medicine or artichoke hearts," I said. "It won't make me well, and it isn't good for me. It's girl stuff, and I don't want any."

"You NEED some," she said. "Don't tell me you haven't noticed how you're growing up."

I just glared at her.

"You're a very pretty girl, Jenelle," Mom told me. "Pretty and a girl. Girls need, want, and have things like panty hose, bras, fancy undies, nail polish, makeup, and pretty clothes."

This is worse than I thought, I told myself glumly. She's not stopping with underwear. This is going on and on, all the way to girls' clothes!

"Now, Mom," I said, trying to sound reasonable. "I know you don't like having a girl who doesn't get excited about all that, but believe me, I'm just not interested in girl stuff. I'll take the egg, here, but let's stop at that. Okay?"

"Do you really think I don't like having you?" Mom asked, looking horrified.

16

"I know you love me," I assured her. "That's pretty automatic with parents, I guess. But I know you wish I was more like Stacy. I'm just not, okay?"

Mom shook her head at me. "Listen, young lady," she said. "I do love you — just exactly as you are. You exasperate me plenty, that's true, but I don't care if you don't like girl stuff."

"You don't?" I was absolutely amazed! Then why were we having an argument about underwear and nail polish?

"I don't," she repeated. "I don't care that you don't like them, and I am delighted that you have found things you do enjoy. Football is great for girls. You can loathe and despise bras and pretty clothes all you want, and I won't care a bit. And I don't want you to be like Stacy. She's a nice girl. She's very grown-up, and I'm glad you're friends. But one Stacy is enough."

"Then let's go home!" I said, relieved.

Mom gave me a funny smile. "You can hate girl things," she said. "But you're going to have them."

All I could do was stare at her with my mouth hanging open in surprise. "Why?" I finally managed to ask.

"Because that way you have options," she said. "If you never wear girl things because you don't own any, then wearing girl things is not an option. If you own them and choose not to wear them,

17

then it's a choice on your part. I want you to have the choice."

I was sure there was something wrong with that argument, but I couldn't figure out what.

So when we finally got home Saturday afternoon I carried a huge bag to my room. I had a hairband, ribbons, and barrettes. I had nail polish. I had a new necklace, perfume, and bath powder. I had a fancy mirror, lipstick, eyeshadow, mascara, and panty hose.

I also had a pair of dress shoes, a frilly blouse, and a skirt. I had two sets of silky undies with matching bras.

And my new socks.

And a new NFL T-shirt — the Giants.

I put my socks in my top dresser drawer, hung the T-shirt in the closet, and put everything else in the bottom drawer of my desk, the one I use to store junk in.

I decided I would wear my new Giants shirt tomorrow, and debated whether to call Stacy and tell her how crazy my mother was.

I finally decided not to. She wouldn't see my mother's behavior as crazy!

I did call her, though. We needed to discuss plans for our birthday parties.

5.
Leave the Football Home

Stacy's birthday is the twenty-seventh of October, and mine is the tenth of November. We have separate parties, but we plan them together every year.

"I'd like to have a boy-girl dancing party," Stacy said dreamily.

I could guess why. She hasn't had much chance to talk with him, but she's been crazy about Mark Turner since the first day he was in our class. That's only been four days, but I know Stacy. She's building herself up to being madly in love with him. She does that several times a year. It's the one thing I find hardest to understand about her!

And I was building myself up to madly disliking him, since he'd taken over for me at quarterback!

"Did you hear me?" Stacy asked.

"I heard you," I said. I was lying on the couch,

with the phone to my ear, my head on one of our big TV pillows, and my feet on another. I had a bowl of salsa dip balanced on my stomach, a bag of potato chips, and a can of pop on the floor right next to the couch.

Mom would lecture me if she saw me. She'd lecture about healthy snacks, lecture about how rude it is to chomp and talk, and lecture about remembering to clean up after eating in the family room.

But she won't see me. She's cleaning out her closet. She does that once a year, and it takes forever because she tries everything on before deciding whether to keep it or get rid of it.

"So what do you think?" Stacy asked.

"About having boys at your party or about dancing?" I asked.

"Dancing," she said.

I munched another chip. "If it makes you happy, do it," I advised.

"Will you dance?" she asked.

"Who cares?" I said. "If there are boys there, I'll have fun." She can dance with Mark, I thought. That'll keep him busy, and I'll have my team back. She's got those spotlights in the backyard, so even if it's night we can still play.

"Jenelle!" Stacy sounded disgusted. "I didn't ask if you'd play football with the boys! I asked if you'd dance with them!"

"Does that mean you don't want me to bring

the ball at all?" I asked suspiciously.

"Oh, would you mind?" Stacy asked. She sounded relieved. "I didn't want to ask you not to, but if you're willing to volunteer, that's different! I should have known you'd understand! If you bring the ball, you and the boys will toss it back and forth all night and ignore the rest of the girls."

The way I remembered it, I hadn't exactly volunteered to leave my football home! And what would I do all night long without it? Maybe I could stay home. Could I do that to my best friend? Probably not. I was probably stuck going.

"Have you picked a day for your party?" I asked.

"November first," she said. "Halloween is on a Friday. Of course I'm not going trick-or-treating. That's too childish for sixth grade. But I know a lot of the boys will go, so if I have my party the day after, I won't interfere with anyone's Halloween plans."

"I guess I'll have mine the following Saturday, then," I said. I was feeling a little bit insulted. Stacy knew I was going trick-or-treating! "And if you're having a dancing party, maybe I'll have a football party." And I won't invite Mark, I thought.

I was only teasing, actually, but I liked the idea as soon as I said it. Besides, it would serve her right for calling me childish.

"Oh, brother!" Stacy said. "Really, Jenelle!"

"If you're having the kind of party I think is awful, it's only fair for me to have the kind you think is awful. Right?"

"But you didn't say you thought it would be awful!" Stacy wailed.

"You knew what I'd think of the idea," I pointed out. "And I didn't complain. I even said I'd leave my football at home."

There was a stubborn silence on the other end of the phone. Then Stacy said, "I guess if you participate fully in my party, I could handle going to a football party."

"What does participate fully mean?" I asked.

"You know," Stacy said. "Come dressed up in a dress and panty hose, with your hair fixed and all. And dance. With boys."

She sounded triumphant, like she was sure I'd back down about my party.

And in fact, the idea of dressing up and dancing sounded pretty awful to me. I'd rather stay home than do that, even if it would hurt Stacy's feelings! But I can get stubborn, too. And after all, Mom had just bought me all the stuff Stacy said I'd need.

"Well," I said. "I guess if you participate fully in my football party, I can handle dressing up and dancing for your party."

"What does participate fully mean for a football

party?" Stacy asked, sounding like she really didn't want to know.

"Oh, you know," I said. "Wearing jeans and a football shirt and playing football. With a football."

"PLAY football?" Stacy asked. "I thought we'd WATCH a game! I could maybe handle that. Jenelle, you know I can't play football!"

"And you know I can't dance," I said. "So we're even."

There was another long pause.

I sighed. "I'll tell you what," I said, breaking the silence. "I'll teach you to play football if you'll teach me to dance."

Stacy sighed, too. "I suppose it won't kill me," she admitted. "You're on. It's a deal."

After I hung up I went to find Mom. She was in her room amid heaps of clothes.

I plopped on the bed, watching her try things on. I told her about Stacy's and my plans for our parties. Mom thought it was pretty funny.

"You both outsmarted yourselves, didn't you?" she said, laughing.

I nodded. "It just popped into my head," I admitted. "I hadn't planned it at all. But do you think I could?"

"Have a football party? I don't see why not."

"It would be easy to decorate the house for it," I said. "I could hang up all my NFL posters and have balloons in team colors by each poster. I could loan an NFL T-shirt to anyone who doesn't have one. Could we find a football cake?"

"Sure," she said. "And I'll bet we can rent a videotape of the best NFL games or bloopers or something. I've seen little plastic helmets we could use to put nuts and mints in, and you certainly have enough equipment to get a few games going."

"And we'll have Orange Crush to drink," I added. "That's what Bronco fans drink. And dog biscuits!"

"Dog biscuits! Whatever for?"

"The Cleveland Browns fans throw dog biscuits," I said. "It's a tradition. And Gatorade. Lots of teams pour Gatorade on the coach's head when they win."

"I don't think we need Gatorade," Mom said quickly. "I don't want people to think they're supposed to dump it on anyone's head!"

"I guess we can do without that," I agreed.

"If you're going to be playing football, you'll want an afternoon party so you have daylight for the game," Mom said. "Will you want me to feed everybody dinner, too?"

"We will get hungry," I told her. "It takes a lot of energy to play football."

"I suppose I could make a football dinner," Mom said. "Let's see. You take one football and put it in a pan of boiling water. Cook for twenty minutes and serve on a bed of noodles."

I started giggling, thinking how Stacy's face would look if Mom put a stewed football on the table. Pretty soon Mom and I were both laughing so hard we got hiccups.

And then Dad walked in.

He looked at Mom in her slip, laughing and hiccuping. He looked at me.

"What's going on?" he asked.

"I've decided I have a pretty neat mother," I told him, between hiccups and giggles. "She may buy me weird underwear, but she sure can cook!"

6.
Invitations

Monday morning Ms. Kennedy called Stacy and me up to her desk and gave us each a long envelope with our name on it.

We opened them as soon as we got back to our seats. Inside mine was a short letter and a badge with a big smiley face on it.

My letter read: *You have been accepted as a bus buddy. Your buddy's name is <u>Sammy Grundy</u>. S/he rides <u>Tuesday & Thursday mornings</u>. Your duties will begin <u>probably next week</u>. Please wear your badge until your buddy knows you.*

I'd been accepted.

Stacy showed me her letter. It said about the same thing except her blanks were filled in <u>Michelle Winder, Monday & Wednesday mornings, Wednesday.</u>

In addition, her letter told her to go down to

the preschool room at eleven-fifteen today to meet her buddy.

And I had to wait until the next week to start work!

But at least I'd been accepted. There were only eleven preschoolers who didn't have older brothers or sisters riding buses with them, and a lot more than eleven sixth-graders had applied. Not everyone got accepted.

I didn't even go near the football game at lunch, waiting instead to talk to Stacy.

"So did you meet her?" I asked when she came outside.

"She's adorable!" Stacy said. "She has curly blonde hair and big blue eyes. She's so CUTE! She came right up to me and held my hand. It was darling!"

Stacy raved about her buddy all day. She gets a little bit self-centered when she gets excited. It's as if what's happening to her is all that matters. She forgets that other people have opinions and feelings, too.

My opinion was, I was getting tired of hearing about her buddy! And my feelings were — left out! I was left out of the football games and left out of the excitement of being a buddy.

But at least I have a buddy, I kept reminding myself. And at least Stacy and I ride different buses. I won't have to watch her sitting with Michelle while I have no one.

Stacy called after school to rave about Michelle. When she finished doing that, she turned to talking about her party.

"Should I put up decorations?" she asked. "Or is that too childish?"

"Do you want decorations?" I asked.

"I don't know!" she wailed. "I want them if they wouldn't be too childish, and I don't want them if it would make it look like a little kids' party."

"Who are you inviting?" I asked.

"I don't know that, either!" she said, wailing again. "Should I invite the girls and have them each invite a boy they want? Or should I decide which boys the girls would want there?"

"Why not just invite all your friends?" I suggested. "Then everyone you want there will be there."

"Oh, Jenelle!" Stacy said. "You don't understand at all! This is a DANCING party! I have to invite people who will dance with each other!"

I think this is getting too complicated, I thought. I listened while Stacy worried, getting a little worried myself. Stacy was making an awfully big deal out of this party, and the more she talked, the worse I thought it sounded.

When Mom and Dad got home from work, Mom handed me a brown paper bag. Inside were party invitations shaped like footballs.

"Great!" I said. "Thanks!"

Except now I'm the one who has to figure out

who to invite, I realized. Stacy isn't the only one with that problem.

I had time before the Monday night game to make a list of people. There were four boys I usually play football with, and another five who joined in sometimes.

I was inviting Stacy, of course. I'd promised to teach her how to play. I finally decided Carly and Andrea would be good sports about a football party. I knew I was not inviting Mark. And that was as far as I could get.

The next morning the bus driver pointed out Sammy's house as we drove by. There was nothing unusual about it. It was red brick, with brownish shutters. It had a tricycle outside, and a basketball hoop set up by the garage.

I wondered how long his mother would keep driving Sammy to school. Since my buddy duties wouldn't start until she got tired of driving him, I hoped it would happen pretty soon.

The chocolate chip cookies are all gone, too, I reminded myself. Better make some more.

When I met Stacy before school, she was still worried about her party. I was getting kind of tired of the subject.

Finally I said, "Look, Stace. I am not the boy-girl dancing party expert. Right?"

Stacy agreed.

"Then my opinion is not exactly worth much, is it?"

Stacy thought about that. "I see your point," she said.

"Good," I told her. I hoped that would change the subject.

"We need to set a time for your dancing lessons, too, don't forget," Stacy said.

"The football lessons are more important, don't you think?" I asked hopefully.

"No," she said. "But I agreed. How about tonight? We can start with dancing lessons, and work up to football lessons."

I nodded, though I had serious doubts about two things: one, that I could learn to dance, and two, that Stacy could learn to play football.

7.
Trading Lessons

Stacy and I only live six blocks apart, though we ride different buses, so after I got home I left a note for my parents, helped myself to a bag of Chee-tos to eat on the way, grabbed my Nerf football, and headed over to her house.

We went down to her basement, which is finished into rooms. The big room, where we were, is where her party was going to be, too.

Stacy put on a record and started dancing. "Just do what I do," she said, moving and spinning in what looked like a very complicated dance. "That's all there is to it."

"Right," I said glumly, watching her. Her dark curls were bouncing, and her face looked serious as she moved to the beat of the music. She looked like a natural.

I feel like a clod when I try to dance. I feel like I'm all arms and legs, and neither arms nor legs

31

know what to do. Stacy had tried to teach me once before, in fourth grade, but it had been a disaster.

"Come on," Stacy urged. "Try it."

"You have to SHOW me how," I said.

"I AM showing you," she said. "Do this."

"If you're going to teach someone, you have to slow things down," I complained. "You have to explain the basics."

Stacy stopped dancing, looking impatient. I can tell this is going to be another one of those lessons, I thought.

"Start easy, okay?" I said. "Take it a little at a time."

"This is music," Stacy said, giving me an exaggerated look of innocence.

"Got that," I said.

"And music has a beat."

"Right, Stace," I said, glaring a little. "I even remember how Mr. Ross used to make us clap our hands to the beat."

"When you dance, you move to the beat."

"Stacy! I know all that. Show me what to move and how to move it!" And quit trying to act grown-up! I added silently. I really don't like Stacy much when she acts like that.

"Feet," Stacy said, pointing. "Move them like this."

She moved hers slowly, back and forth. I was almost mad enough to quit, but it looked easy, so I tried it.

She moved faster, and I had to watch more closely.

"That's it," Stacy encouraged.

She didn't sound impatient anymore, and I was glad. I didn't want to fight with her.

"Now sway a little," Stacy directed. "No, not like that. Like this."

"What are my hands supposed to be doing?" I asked.

She showed me a few things hands and arms could do, and I copied her.

"Good!" she said, laughing. "You can dance."

"I still feel dumb," I told her. "Don't I look kind of klutzy?"

Stacy watched me a minute, her face serious. I felt dumber and dumber.

"You do look a little jerky," she said finally. "But that's just because you haven't had much practice. The movements don't feel natural to you. Keep doing it, and they will."

"Now for slow dancing," I said.

"Oh, that's easy," Stacy said. "The girl puts one hand on the guy's shoulder, he puts one hand on your waist and you hold hands with the leftover hands. You both move your feet back and forth at the same time."

Stacy put on a slow song and showed me. She was right. It was easy, although I stepped on her feet a few times.

She put on a fast record again, and we practiced

a while longer. Then she got us each a can of Pepsi, and we collapsed on the couch, gulping thirstily. Dancing is hard work!

"I'd better have lots to drink at my party," Stacy said. Then she added, "I'm sorry I got mad, Jenelle. I just don't like being criticized."

I was surprised. Stacy didn't usually apologize. Usually she was convinced she'd been right, and I was the one who wound up apologizing.

"I wasn't criticizing you," I said. "Just your rotten teaching."

Stacy tossed a couch cushion at my face. I tossed it back.

"Anyway," I said, tipping my head back and holding the Pepsi can upside down above my mouth to get the last drops. "Don't feel badly if I'm never a great dancer. It won't be your teaching. It'll just be because I'm a klutzy student."

"You looked good," she insisted. "Honest. You can dance just fine. Just practice until you feel comfortable."

I squashed my can and tossed it through the air. It sailed up in a beautiful arc, landing perfectly in the recycling bin. "Football time!" I announced.

Stacy groaned. "Can't it wait?" she asked hopefully. "We've already had enough exercise for today."

"That was just a warm-up," I said. "Besides, football is complicated. You'll need several lessons to understand the game and to practice the plays. And we've only got a couple of weeks."

She groaned again, but she stood up. She walked over and put her can in the bin, then faced me with a trapped look on her face.

·"I'm ready," she said.

I have to admit Stacy's a good sport. She looked like she was being hauled off to prison, not just outside to toss a football, and she was trying to smile about it. That's definitely a good sport!

The first thing I showed Stacy was how to hold a football. "Spread your fingers here," I explained. "Your thumb goes on the other side. Come on, it won't bite."

Stacy held the ball as if it might go off any second, or as if it didn't smell very good.

"Now, drop your hand back . . . no, bend your arm at the elbow."

It didn't take long to understand how Stacy felt when I criticized her teaching. It isn't easy to figure out why something is hard for someone else, when it's almost second nature to you!

I had to take every motion apart into six or seven simpler ones. I had to teach her how to make each of the simpler moves, then how to put them all back together into one smooth action.

By the time I had to go home, Stacy had learned to hold the ball properly, to put her arm in position for throwing, and that was it. She simply couldn't throw. Her elbow kept sticking way out to the side, and she'd clip her ear with the ball as she tried to release it.

Stacy was so discouraged she was nearly in tears.

"Don't worry," I told her. I was nearly as discouraged as she was, but I tried not to show it. "It's like learning to ride a bike. It's hard at first, but it all comes together. You'll see. You'll do fine."

"Right, fine," I muttered later, walking home. "Fine if we need someone who can throw the ball straight down on the ground in front of them."

Maybe we should work on catching and running and strategy, I thought. Stacy can forget blocking. She's too small. But she'd make a good receiver if she could learn to catch.

But that would require more lessons. And what about Andrea and Carly?

"Mom?" I asked at dinner. We were having spaghetti and French bread, which Mom cooks pretty good, but Dad cooks fantastically. Luckily Dad was *On For Dinner* tonight, so we were all busy stuffing ourselves, hardly saying a word.

"Yes?" Mom asked, when I didn't continue.

I'd taken another huge bite just as I got her attention, so I had to chew and swallow before I finished my question.

"Do you think I could have Stacy, Andrea, and

Carly spend the night Friday?" I asked. "We need to have a football clinic."

Mom started laughing so hard she almost choked. She took a drink of water and tried to look serious, but her eyes kept laughing even though she'd stopped.

"That's my Jenelle!" she told me. "A football clinic! I can just see it now. Jenelle lines all the girls up, shouting, 'We're gonna win this game!' and the girls will chant, 'Right, Coach. Win! Win!' and you'll say, 'Stacy, you can't go to bed till you can throw that ball!' "

Dad was grinning, too. I had to admit the idea would probably be just as funny to my friends as it was to Mom.

But they'll be grateful for a little help with the game so they can play at my football party, I decided. They won't want to look like idiots in front of the boys.

"Well, can I?" I asked.

Mom looked thoughtful. "I guess I can accomplish my Saturday errands without you," she said. "Okay. If you make up any chores you miss, and if you clean up after your guests."

"All right!" I cheered. "Dad, will you help with the clinic?"

"Sure," he agreed. "I'm available on Saturday. I'll even help Friday night if you help me with the dishes."

"Deal!" I shouted. Dad's really good at calling

plays and coaching, and he's very patient when he teaches. He taught me to play, so he ought to be able to teach my friends, too.

"Will you ref at my football party game?" I asked him.

"Aren't you worried I might favor the other team?" he teased.

I grinned at him. "I might offer a small bribe," I said. "Like, say, I do dishes all week next time you're *On For Dinner*?"

"Bribing the official will get you kicked out of the league!" he said. "You'll never play again!"

"Oh, darn," I said, acting disappointed. "I guess you'll just have to do your own dishes."

8.
She's So Cute

The next day, Wednesday, Stacy started her bus buddy duties.

"She's so CUTE!" Stacy raved when we met on the playground before school. "She held my hand the whole way, and chattered on and on. She calls me 'Tacy,' and it's just darling the way she says it! She had on the ruffliest dress I ever saw, all pink and white, and she had a pink bow in her hair. She's adorable!"

I was glad when Ms. Kennedy started the English lesson. Hearing about troublesome teasers like *its* and *it's*, *their*, *there*, and *they're*, and *to*, *too*, and *two* was better than hearing *CUTE* one more time!

She assigned us a worksheet for homework. We were supposed to write twenty-five sentences showing how to use each teaser properly. Then she handed me an envelope and started the math lesson. Fractions.

I ripped open the envelope. There was a letter from Mrs. Benson inside. It read: *Dear Jenelle, Sorry you won't get a chance to meet your bus buddy before your duties begin. Mrs. Grundy called this morning. She'd like you to help Sammy beginning tomorrow morning. Your bus driver knows which stop is his. Thank you.*

I almost cheered! Tomorrow morning I'd be a buddy! I couldn't wait!

"Jenelle, do you understand the concept?"

"Oh, yes. He'll be adorable!" As soon as the words left my mouth I could feel my face getting hot. Had I really said that? I slithered down in my seat while everyone snickered at me.

"No," Ms. Kennedy said, hiding a smile. "Adorable has nothing to do with fractions. The point is, the larger the bottom number is, the smaller the size of the piece. One eighth is smaller than one quarter, even though eight is a larger number than four."

"Right," I managed to agree.

"And the top number?" she prompted.

"Tells how many pieces you're talking about," I said.

"Good," she said.

She went on with the lesson, and I listened this time, making myself forget about my buddy. I didn't want to be embarrassed like that again.

"Who's adorable?" everyone kept asking me at lunch.

I'm not sure they believed my answer. A bus buddy wasn't nearly as exciting to them as the hope that I'd developed a crush on someone. I could have told them that Orange Crush was about as crushy as I was likely to get.

At lunch Stacy and I watched the boys play, and Stacy was watching the game, not just Mark. I know because she asked me lots of questions.

"Why did Mark get so mad when Jason caught the ball?" she asked. "I thought people were supposed to catch it."

"Jason was on the other team," I explained. "Mark was throwing to Saul and Jason caught it instead. That's an interception."

"Well, why didn't Jason let Saul get the ball if it was supposed to be for Saul?" she asked.

"You want to score, Stacy," I explained. "You have to have the ball to score."

"Then why isn't everyone grabbing at the ball all the time?" Stacy asked. "When everybody lined up so nicely someone could have grabbed the ball from Bobby before he handed it to Mark."

"The play hadn't started," I said. "Until Bobby actually hands off the ball, no one else can take it, unless Bobby fumbles, of course."

"Oh."

I was delighted at Stacy's interest, and I figured this was a good time to explain the game to her.

41

She could watch the guys play while I told her what they were doing and why.

"See," I said, "when you're at the line of scrimmage, it's like you're waiting for a race to begin. It begins when the ball is snapped. Bobby hands it to Mark, and Mark drops back to pass. See? The other team is rushing him, trying to get a sack. Look, Bobby is guarding Mark, and see those guys running downfield? They're receivers. They're trying to catch the pass. They'll keep playing until the play is dead, like if the ball hits the ground, or there's a score."

"You lost me at the line of scrimmage," Stacy said sadly. "There weren't any lines on that field at all."

This was going to be harder than I thought!

"Let's back up," I said, sketching a football field in the sand. "Here's the field, see?"

Stacy nodded.

"This half," I said, drawing in the fifty-yard line, "is mine." It is when I'm the quarterback, anyway, I thought. "The other half is the other team's. If I'm going to score, I have to do it here, clear on the far end of the other guys' side."

"Got it," Stacy said.

"When it's my team's turn with the ball, our job is to get as far into enemy territory as we can, while the other team's job is to keep us from getting there."

"Makes sense," Stacy said.

"I'm the offense when I have the ball," I said. "That's when I'm trying to get into their territory. This side is the defense, because they're defending their territory. When it's my turn with the ball, I have four tries to make ten yards."

"Why?"

"Because if we make ten yards, we get four more turns to try going ten more yards. Where we start is called the line of scrimmage, and each turn with the ball is called a down."

Stacy scratched her head. "Let's talk about something else now," she suggested. "Like, what are you wearing to my party?"

"How about my Washington Redskins shirt?" I asked.

She whacked my arm. "Absolutely not!" she said, "Get serious, okay?"

"Okay," I agreed. "I'll wear the Vikings."

She hit me again. "Jenelle!" she said sternly.

"Mom got me some stuff," I said. "A skirt and a top. I'll wear that."

"What does it look like?"

The bell rang, so we headed back toward the building.

"It's mostly black, I think," I said. "With kind of swirly designs. Maybe it's actually dark blue. I think there's a ruffle or something on it, too."

Stacy shook her head at my description.

"I put it away!" I protested. "I haven't looked at it since I got it. How do I know what it looks like? Mom mostly picked it out, anyway."

"Do you at least know it fits?" she asked as we walked into the classroom.

"I tried it on," I said. "It fits."

9.
My Buddy

I dreamed about my buddy that night.
He was so cute!

I didn't actually see Sammy in my dream, but I knew he was cute. I was riding the bus in my new skirt and my frilly blouse, and Mrs. Grundy kept saying how grown-up I looked. She handed me a little doll all wrapped up in a towel and told me to take good care of her baby. Then she told me I could keep him.

It was an odd dream, and I laughed when I woke up.

Then I got nervous. What if Mrs. Grundy didn't think I could do a good job? It would be very embarrassing if she called the preschool teacher and told her I wasn't mature enough to take care of her little boy.

I decided the dream idea of dressing up was probably a good one. I'd look older and more responsible. Mom and Dad dressed up to go to work. Mom had explained that people judge you by how you dress, which doesn't seem fair, but if that's how it is, that's how it is. Fair or not.

Reluctantly, I took off my Chicago Bears T-shirt and my jeans, putting on a pair of slacks and a long-sleeved button-down striped shirt with a sweater over it. The outfit was a present from my grandparents, for school. I'd never worn it.

When I showed up for breakfast, my parents both stared, too shocked to speak. As a matter of fact, they didn't say a word about my clothes. Mom gave me a kiss when she left, and I could tell she was feeling my forehead for fever.

She gave me a half-worried look, but all she said was, "Have a good day, and I'll see you at five."

Dad just raised his eyebrows and kissed the top of my head. Then they both rushed off.

I had my usual school-morning breakfast of toast, banana, and instant hot chocolate. Then I rinsed my dishes and my parents' dishes and put them all in the dishwasher. Since I have more time in the mornings than my parents do, I'm *On For A.M. K.P. Duty* Monday through Friday. My parents take over Kitchen Patrol on the weekends.

I wiped the table and the counters, made my lunch, gathered my things, and went out to the bus stop.

I was still nervous. What if Sammy didn't like

me? What if he started crying and wouldn't hold my hand?

The bus came and we all got on.

"You know my buddy's supposed to ride this morning, right?" I asked the driver.

"Yes," she told me. "When I stop, you just go ahead on over and get him."

"Okay."

Finally we were there. I could see a woman in slacks and a gray jacket standing in the front yard. She held a little kid by the hand, but I couldn't see much of him except a fuzzy blue coat and a fuzzy blue hat and mittens.

The bus doors hissed open, and I zipped down the steps, waited for the driver to wave me across, and then I was face-to-face with my buddy's mother. She wasn't much taller than I am, and she seemed just as nervous.

"I'm Jenelle," I said to her. "Hi, Sammy," I told the fuzzy blue bundle.

"Hi." His answer was muffled because his coat collar was turned up to keep the wind off his face.

I didn't think it was cold enough for all that coat and hat and mittens on one little boy, even if October mornings are nippy. I just had on a light-weight jacket.

"He's had a cold," Mrs. Grundy explained. "He can unbundle on the bus, but he needs to be all wrapped up again before he gets off at school."

"Okay," I said. "Let's go, Sammy. He'll be fine,"

I added, in case his mom needed reassuring.

I held the mittened hand and walked him back across the street, helped him up the steps, which are awfully big for a little kid, and showed him where we'd be sitting.

I boosted him up onto the seat, and as soon as I was sitting, too, the bus started off. I helped Sammy, who was trying to tug his mittens off. Then he pulled his hat off and looked up at me, his big brown eyes lighting up with recognition.

"You's the six-grader," he said, enormously pleased.

And he was the little angel who had kicked me because I let the blond have his ball back!

I couldn't believe it! Of all the kids in the world to choose a buddy from, I had to get him! I groaned. I considered quitting my job right then.

Sammy smiled at me.

He really is adorable, I thought. Maybe he won't be that bad.

Sammy smiled again. He looked so angelic I could almost forget the kick, even though he'd put a lot of power into it. His eyes lit up when he smiled.

He'd folded his collar down, lopsided, so he had blue fuzzy behind one ear, and not behind the other. His cheeks were rosy, and he looked very proud to be on the bus. I realized I'd forgotten to pack him some cake. I'd have to remember to bring something next time.

He spent most of the ride looking out the window, watching quietly. I relaxed. It might work out, I told myself.

As we neared the school, Sammy looked at me again, his eyes worried.

"Will my teacha be there?" he asked.

"Yes," I promised. "She meets the bus."

He snuggled his hand into mine, and I relaxed a little more. He was awfully cute. His hand was wet. He must be nervous, I thought.

There's a sharp curve that's about a block from the school. After we went around it, I told Sammy we needed to bundle him back up.

He shook his head.

"Your mom said so," I reminded him.

He shook his head.

There wasn't much point in arguing. I reached around him on the seat to get his mittens, then let go of his hand so I could put the mittens on him. My hand felt wet and slimy. I looked at it, then I looked at him.

"What is all over your hands?" I asked.

"Snot," he said.

I looked at my hand again. I wanted to smear it all over his angelic little face.

I guess my feelings showed, because Sammy rummaged through his coat pocket until he found a rumpled tissue and handed it to me.

I wiped my hand, then wiped his hand, then wiped his nose. The tissue was pretty disgusting.

"Here," I said, holding it out to him.

He shook his head.

By that time the bus was parked and emptying out. I grabbed his hat, forced myself to hold onto the tissue instead of dropping it into his hat like I felt like doing, and jammed the hat on Sammy's head, which he was still shaking "no" at me.

I flipped his collar up, grabbed his mittens, and pushed him off the seat into the aisle.

"Hol' my han'!" he demanded.

"Not unless it has a mitten on it," I told him firmly.

Quickly he held out his hands, and I slipped the mittens on fast. Then I got him off the bus and handed him over to Mrs. Benson.

"How'd it go?" she asked.

I wanted to tell her exactly how it had gone, snotty hands and all, but I bit back my words, smiled, and said, "Fine."

His teacher looked relieved. "Oh, good," she said. "Sammy can be a little stubborn sometimes."

10.
The Clinic

Mom was wrong. I didn't line everybody up and yell at them.

I divided us into two groups with a football per group, and had everyone tossing and catching, moving apart as far as they could and still catch the ball. For Stacy, that wasn't very far.

Actually, Carly and Andrea weren't bad at tossing and catching, especially after they'd practiced a while. They looked very serious, concentrating. Carly has short, curly brown hair and bright blue eyes. Andrea has short red hair and is usually dressed in the latest style. Neither of them usually plays any physical game, especially not football, but they were doing fine.

I told them to keep practicing and to try running out, turning and catching passes on the run.

I worked with Stacy. She had a tendency to shy away from the ball. When she saw it coming, she'd duck back or dodge to the side and hold an arm up to shield her face.

"It's a Nerf ball," I called to her. "It won't hurt. Let it hit you a few times and you'll see."

Stacy put her fists on her hips and turned to glare at me.

"Let it HIT me? On PURPOSE?"

"Sure," I said. "So you can see it won't hurt."

I threw the ball directly at her, and since she was still glaring at me with her hands on her hips, the ball hit her right in the face.

"Oh, yuck!" she yelled. "It tastes awful!"

"Keep your mouth shut, then," I called. "Toss it back."

She was so mad she picked the ball up and tried to hit me with it . . . and almost did!

"You've got it!" I shouted. "You threw it right to me! Try it again."

I lobbed her an easy pass, which she didn't catch, but she did pick it up and throw it back — right to me again.

"All right!" I cheered. "Stacy, you're great!"

She looked doubtful, but after that I noticed she showed more interest in what we were doing. She really listened when I explained how to use the ball's momentum to pull it toward her chest as she caught it, and how to cradle it as she ran so she wouldn't drop it.

Stacy will never be a great football player, but by the time my parents got home she had definitely improved. She was an almost acceptable catcher and a decent passer.

We were exhausted. I hadn't realized how hard I'd been working everyone. We crowded around my dad in the kitchen, begging for food.

"I'm starved!" I told him.

"Famished!" Andrea said.

"We're all going to die if we don't get fed," Carly said.

"Okay, I get the hint!" Dad told us, laughing. "Get out of the kitchen so I can work. I'll put on a hustle, and we'll have burritos in a half hour."

"You can knock that down to fifteen minutes with our help," I said.

Dad looked thoughtful for all of two seconds before agreeing.

"Jenelle, dig in that cupboard until you find the green chile sauce, the refried beans, and the salsa," he ordered. "Stacy, you know our fridge pretty well. You find cheese, lettuce, tomato, and the tortillas. Carly, you set the table, and Andrea, you chop and shred."

He had us organized and out of each other's way in no time. It actually took eighteen minutes to get dinner on the table, but when you're starving, that's much better than a half hour!

"Thank heaven for microwaves and helpers," Dad told us. "That's the fastest dinner I've ever cooked!"

It disappeared fast, too.

Dad decided it was too dark to practice outside after we did the dishes, so he suggested discussing strategy and plays instead.

"You still have a chalkboard somewhere, don't you?" he asked me.

I skipped off to find it and when I got back, Dad had my friends in a circle on the floor, listening while he explained the duties of the players.

"Protect your quarterback," he said. "And make yards. Those are the two most important things when it's your ball. Naturally, the other team is going to be trying its best to keep you from doing that."

Dad crouched like he was on the line, waiting for the snap. Then he rushed at me, and I barely had time to drop the chalkboard before he had me flat on the floor.

"I just sacked your quarterback!" Dad announced.

"You didn't get my flag!" I told him, laughing. "Personal foul. Fifteen yards."

"Tackling is too dangerous," Dad explained. "So we don't do it."

The girls looked relieved.

"We use flags instead," I told them. "Like a bandana tucked into your waistband. You grab the person's flag and yank it off instead of tackling."

Dad set up the chalkboard and drew a play on it, using circles to show the players and arrows to show their movements. While he explained, I watched my friends' faces.

They're interested! I realized, relieved. They're not just being polite. They're really interested!

Dad explained three plays to them, showing what they were supposed to do if they were on offense, how to recognize the play and defend against it if they were on defense.

Then he leaned the chalkboard against the wall and brushed his hands together to knock the chalkdust off them.

"Enough football for tonight," he announced, and the girls actually groaned.

"You'll have to eat popcorn or watch TV or do some other horrible thing," he told us. "I quit for tonight. See you on the field after breakfast."

"Thanks, Mr. Miller," Carly told him. "That was fun."

"I didn't know the game was so complicated," Stacy said to me. "I thought you guys were just running around and tossing the ball back and forth."

"Let's dance," Andrea suggested.

A few days ago I would have done something else while they danced, but I just winked at Stacy and turned on the radio, spinning the station dial until I heard a good beat.

Then we danced. I watched Carly and Andrea and imitated their movements, too, until I felt more comfortable and not so klutzy. They each did a few things different from each other, and a few that were the same.

It's not so hard, I decided. It's not nearly as hard as I thought it was. It's not even as hard as football. You don't have as many rules to follow, and you don't have to worry about fouling someone, either.

"I can't wait for your party," Carly said to Stacy. "Is Jason coming?"

"He sounded kind of scared to come, if you ask me," Stacy said. "But I think he will because Mark's coming. And so are Kyle and Saul and Bobby."

"How about Brad?" Andrea asked. "And José?"

"I don't know," Stacy admitted. "I asked them. And I asked Matthew, Chris, Todd, Gabe, and Brent, too. So far they haven't said if they're coming or not."

"I hope they all come," Andrea said. "That would be fun."

"It will be fun if people dance," Stacy said. "Instead of sitting around like lumps."

"Like couch potatoes," I said, thinking of the lunch football games I'd missed because of Mark. Except for the few times Dad and I had tossed a ball around, watching games was as close as I seemed to be getting to them these days. But I'd get my revenge at my party. No Mark. Just me and the guys again.

"What?" Andrea asked.

"Couch potatoes," I repeated.

That made everybody laugh because they all know I sit and watch the games all season.

"But I don't always sit on the couch," I protested. "Sometimes I'm a floor potato, or a pillow potato."

"Baked, french-fried, or boiled?" Carly asked.

"Raw, I think. And sprouting eyes and getting all old and wrinkled."

"And squishy," Stacy added. "Old potatoes are squishy."

By the time we finished laughing Mom showed up with two huge bowls of buttered popcorn. She sent me off after napkins and soft drinks, and then we all attacked the popcorn, scooping big handfuls out of the bowl and cramming them into our mouths.

In between mouthfuls, I asked, "What's a down?"

"What you get from ducks!" Stacy called.

Carly giggled, and a soggy kernel of popcorn fell from her mouth onto the carpet. That set everyone off again.

Finally Andrea said, "You get four tries to move the ball ten yards. Each try is a down."

"Right!" I said. "What's a sack? And don't tell me it's a bag to put garbage in."

"It's when the other team gets your quarterback after the snap but before he passes the ball or hands it off to someone," Andrea said.

"Or she," Stacy said. "Jenelle's a she."

And sometimes she's a quarterback, I thought, but I said, "Right!" again. "What's a touchback?"

"I know!" Stacy shouted. "It's when you kick off to the other team, and the ball goes into the end zone. It's brought out to the twenty-yard line!"

"Hooray for you!" I said. "What's a quarterback?"

"Mark," Stacy said dreamily. "He's so cute!"

"That wasn't what I meant," I said. But the conversation turned to boys, and football was forgotten.

"Mark said hi to me today," Stacy said.

"Stacy, would you kiss him?" Andrea asked.

Stacy turned red. "I might," she admitted.

"I'd be scared to kiss a boy," Andrea told her. "I wouldn't know what to do."

"I'd like to learn," Carly said.

"How about you, Jenelle?" Andrea asked.

"I'd play football with any of them," I said.

They groaned at me. "Don't you ever think of boys without thinking of football, too?" Andrea asked.

I thought for a minute, then shook my head. "What can I say?" I asked. "Some boys are nice and fun to be around, some aren't. Some enjoy football, some don't. I enjoy the ones who enjoy football."

"Don't you ever think about kissing?" Stacy

asked. "Don't you ever want to have a boyfriend and fall in love?"

I didn't have to think for long. I shook my head. "Nope."

"You are weird!" Stacy said. "Of course, maybe that's why I like you. I must be attracted to weirdness."

"Yeah, like Mark," Andrea said. "He's definitely weird!"

They continued talking about boys, but I ignored the conversation, frowning and thinking.

Is it really so weird that I don't care about kissing? I wondered. I'm not even quite twelve yet. Maybe it's something I'll get interested in later. Stacy says it always happens when people grow up. It's a sign of maturity. Maybe that's true, but if it's going to happen to me, I hope it's not for a long time!

I wondered if everything would change as I grew up. I hoped not! Stacy didn't change. From the time I first met her, all she ever cared about was boys and how she looked. She must have been born that way. Maybe I was born interested in football, and maybe I'd never change.

But that was kind of scary when I thought about it. After all, there isn't much future in NFL football for girls!

I sighed.

"What's wrong?" Stacy asked. "Have you realized what you're missing in life by not kissing?"

"I'll probably live to be ninety-two years old," I said. "Maybe I'll get around to kissing in the next eighty years. I was feeling sad because I know I'll never be a 275-pound linebacker. Darn it, anyway!"

Andrea grabbed her pillow from the pile of overnight stuff we'd stacked in the family room. She whacked me with it.

I grabbed my pillow and hit her back.

The fight was on. We whapped each other, shrieking and giggling. Finally Stacy got the hiccups from laughing so hard, and we stopped the pillow fight to give her advice.

"Breathe in and out of a paper bag," Andrea told her.

"No. Hold your breath," Carly said.

"The only thing that works is drinking from the wrong side of a cup," I said. "I'll go get a glass of water."

I filled a glass half full of water and gave it to Stacy.

She started to drink.

"No, no!" I said. "You have to drink from the wrong side."

Stacy put the wrong side to her lips, which meant her chin was in the glass. She pulled it away.

"It's . . . *hic* . . . impossible," she said.

"No, it's not," I told her. "Tip the glass up and

water will run onto the roof of your mouth. Then suck it to the back of your throat and swallow it."

Stacy had to bend almost double to get the water in her mouth. Suddenly she lost her balance, shrieked, and fell, throwing a hand out to catch herself before she landed on her head. Naturally she used the hand with the cup in it, and water went flying, splashing Andrea, who was closest.

"Yikes!" Andrea shrieked, too, and jumped back from the water, stepping right into one of the popcorn bowls.

It was almost empty, but it was greasy from the butter and Andrea went down, too.

Stacy sat up, water dripping from her face, and glared at us. Andrea, also dripping, and with her foot all greasy and still in the bowl, glared, too.

Carly and I looked at them, then looked at each other, and collapsed on the floor, laughing all over again.

"It cured your hiccups!" I told Stacy.

"Oh, no! Mrs. Miller, that's rotten!" Stacy shrieked, grabbing her pillow and clamping it over her face.

I looked over and there stood Mom, grinning at us from behind her camera. She chuckled, then waved and went back upstairs like nothing had happened.

"I wonder how long she was standing there,"

Stacy said, emerging from behind her pillow.

"Don't worry," I said. "I don't think she heard you talking about kissing."

Stacy looked relieved.

"Let's clean up this mess," Carly suggested. "Then we can spread out our sleeping bags and watch a late movie."

"Can't watch for too long," I said. "You're in training. You've got to get a good night's sleep if you're going to be playing football tomorrow. And you ARE going to be playing football tomorrow!"

"Yes, coach," Andrea said.

"Coach Couch Potato," I said thoughtfully. "I like it."

We turned on the late movie, which was a pirate movie. It wasn't very realistic, but it wasn't quite bad enough to be funny, either. We got sleepier and sleepier, watching.

The next thing I knew, I was smelling coffee and food.

Saturday morning Dad usually fixes bacon and pancakes, and judging from the smells wafting down to us, this was no exception.

"Mmm," Andrea murmured. "Something smells good!"

I stretched and yawned, and finally crawled out of my sleeping bag.

"I'm going to brush my teeth and stuff, and then go start the hot chocolate," I told Andrea. "You get those guys up, okay?"

I made a paste of cocoa and water, sugar, and a dribble of salt, heated it, then slowly added milk, stirring with a whisk.

By the time I added the vanilla, Dad had a huge plate of pancakes made and a mound of crisp bacon on another plate.

"Food!" he called. "Come and get it!"

Mom set out plates and silverware while my friends helped carry over the food.

I put Cool Whip and marshmallows on the table, carried over the hot chocolate, and joined the crowd for breakfast.

I was sure Dad had cooked way too many pancakes, but before I could mention it, they were half gone. And then I found myself reaching for the last one.

"Don't stuff yourself," Andrea warned. "Remember, we've got practice this morning."

"You're right," I said, leaving the pancake. "I'd better not eat too much if I'm going to be doing all that exercise."

Andrea grabbed the pancake, grinning at me while she ate it.

Dad sent us out to warm up and then had us run out for passes while he fired footballs in all directions. He had us run patterns and still try to catch his passes.

"These are the plays I showed you," he reminded us. "Remember, you fake the other team into thinking you're going to run the ball, then zip upfield and be ready for the pass."

He could really fire those balls! We were playing in the vacant lot across the street from my house. It's full of weeds, but Dad and I filled in the holes years ago and hauled the rocks off, using some to mark the yard lines and goalposts, so it's always ready for playing. It's not anywhere near as big as a real football field, but it's big enough for a friendly game.

After we ran patterns for a while, Dad had us run with the ball, and whoever wasn't carrying it was supposed to chase whoever had it and practice getting flags. That's as close to a scrimmage as we could get with only four players and a ref.

Then Dad had us each be the quarterback and fire balls upfield to each other.

When we finally quit at eleven, we were sweaty, dirty, exhausted, and good!

Even Stacy was good. Not just okay, but good!

"You are wonderful!" I told them all. "We're better than most of the boys.

"Let's not tell anyone about this, okay?" Stacy suggested. "Let's keep it a secret."

"Yeah," Andrea agreed. "We'll just watch the games at lunch, like always. And then when you have your football party, we'll knock their socks off!"

"They won't believe their eyes!" Carly added. "They'll be so shocked when we score all over them!"

"I can't wait for your party!" Andrea said.

I couldn't believe it! Overnight, these three girls had turned into football freaks!

"Can we come over and practice again?" Stacy asked. "We'll need to keep working so we don't forget what we've learned."

I couldn't believe that, either! Stacy, asking to play football?

"Hey, this was great!" Carly said, packing her overnight things. "I can't remember having this much fun in ages."

"Yeah," Andrea agreed. "I loved it. And now when my dad turns into a couch potato on Sunday I can say things about the game that make sense." She finished rolling up her bag and tossed her pillow onto the stack. "Remember not to tell the boys," she added. "It's going to be so much fun when Mark rolls out to make a pass to Jason and I intercept it and run it back for a touchdown!"

Uh-oh, I thought. Andrea expects Mark to be at my party! She expects him to be a quarterback! Everyone will expect him to be there and to be the other quarterback!

"Dream on," Stacy said. "You won't intercept Mark. If anyone does, it'll be me."

"I'm talking ON-the-field action," Andrea teased.

11.
A Job Offer

I was tired. We'd stayed up late, gotten up early, and played hard. I wanted a nap, but I'd promised to clean up after my party, and to catch up on my chores.

I checked the schedule. Friday night I had been *On For Dusting Liv. Rm. and Fam. Rm.* Saturday is odd jobs, besides errands, and Mom wasn't home to assign me any odd jobs, so I got the Pledge and the dust cloth and the pole duster, and dusted corners and tables, knickknacks and pictures, drapes, and lamps in the living room and family room.

Then I vacuumed and took the popcorn bowls up and washed them. That was really all the mess we'd made, except for the chalkboard. I put that away, too.

While I worked, I thought. My friends had

turned into football people so quickly. And easily. Did that mean I could change easily, too? Would I one day, all of a sudden, turn into a Stacy-type who giggled and liked boys and paid more attention to how she looked than to anything else? Did being grown-up mean being like Stacy? That seems to be what Stacy thought.

I shuddered. I hoped not!

I decided to do my homework so I wouldn't have anything to interfere with the games tomorrow. I don't have time for much except football on Sundays. With the early game, the late game, and the pre- and post-game shows, Dad and I spend just about the whole day as couch potatoes, sprouting eyes and getting wrinkled and squishy.

When the phone rang I was in the middle of math homework, so I jumped up eagerly to answer it. Distractions are always welcome during homework time.

"Hello?" I said.

"May I speak to Jenelle?"

"This is Jenelle," I said, surprised to hear a grown-up asking for me.

"This is Mrs. Grundy. Sammy's mother?"

I was suddenly worried. I didn't think I'd done anything wrong with Sammy on Thursday.

"Yes?" I asked. What if she wants to fire me? I thought.

"Sammy's so proud to be riding the bus," Mrs. Grundy said. "He hasn't stopped talking about you since Thursday. He thinks you're wonderful, Jenelle."

"I'm glad he had a good time," I said. At least I'm not in trouble! I told myself.

"I wanted to thank you for being his buddy," Mrs. Grundy said. "But I had another reason for calling. I was wondering, do you think you might be able to take Sammy trick-or-treating on Halloween? I'd pay you, of course."

A paid job? Me?

"Sammy's dad is due back from a business trip the thirty-first," Mrs. Grundy explained. "I have to be at the airport. I don't want Sammy to miss trick-or-treating. He's been so excited about it. It just doesn't seem fair to make him go to the airport with me and miss all the fun."

"I'd love to do it," I said.

"Oh, thank you. That's such a relief. Thank you so much!"

We arranged the details of when I should come to get him on Halloween, and where to take him trick-or-treating, and I hung up the phone feeling excited about my first paid job.

I'm going to get paid for going trick-or-treating! I thought. How lucky can I get?

When mom came home I told her about the phone call. She looked a little shocked.

"I hadn't realized you were old enough to baby-sit," she said. "Do you think you can handle it?"

What's to handle? I thought. I'm an expert at trick-or-treating! All I have to do is take Sammy along with me. "Of course I can handle it," I told Mom. "No problem."

12.
Wums

Tuesday morning, again, I walked across the
street to escort Sammy to the bus. His mother
didn't look nervous this time, and Sammy wasn't
all bundled up. He wore a windbreaker-type
jacket, like I did, and he held a paper bag in one
hand.

Mrs. Grundy gave Sammy a quick kiss. Sammy
ran over to hug me around the legs, his paper bag
crinkling behind me.

In our seat he smiled at me shyly. He really
was cute!

"Got my show-an'-tell," he said a few blocks
later. He patted his bag. It rustled.

"Can I see?" I asked.

He nodded. "Hol' out your han's," he ordered.

I did. I held them out like a cup, both of them
together.

He carefully unfolded the top of the bag, then

turned it upside down over my hands.

"Gah!" I yelped. Dirt and worms came tumbling out all over me. I'd been expecting a couple of Matchbox cars and instead, I had a sudden lapful of garden dirt and what looked like a hundred squiggly worms!

"Ketchum! Ketchum!" Sammy shrieked. "They wunnin' away!"

I could feel the bus driver's eyes boring holes into me in her mirror. I scooped as much of the mess as I could off my lap and into Sammy's paper bag.

"Sssh!" I hissed. "You have to be quiet on the bus!" Why me? I thought. Stacy's buddy would never bring worms to school!

Sammy sniffled and pointed sadly at a worm that had fallen to the floor. I reached down and snagged it up, and then the little girl in the seat in front of us screamed.

"It's all over my shoes! What is it?" she said, sounding horrified.

I knew what it was, but I wasn't saying a word! If Sammy knew she had squished one of his worms, he'd really start crying! The little girl probably wouldn't be too happy, either.

"A worm!"

"Oh, look. Worms!"

There must have been a thousand in that bag. Two little kids found some, then some bigger kids found some and pretty soon they were dropping worms down people's shirts and dangling them in front of people's faces.

I covered my face with my hands, and Sammy howled. I could feel the bus slowing. It stopped.

"What is going on?" The driver didn't sound happy at all.

"Worms!" a little boy told her. "See?" He held out a particularly long, particularly squiggly worm to show her.

"MY WUM!" Sammy screeched. "Give it back!"

The bus driver turned pale and shrank away from the worm the boy was still holding out.

"MINE!" Sammy yelled. His face was turning red.

"Who is responsible for this?" the driver demanded.

"Oh, ick! Get it away from me!" someone yelled.

"MINE! Sammy want my WUM!"

I didn't have a choice. I stood up, holding up the paper bag. "They're Sammy's show-and-tell," I admitted. I swallowed hard. "They spilled. I didn't know he had worms, honest."

"Get all the worms back in the bag! Right now!" the driver ordered us. "Every one of them. Go on. Now!"

"Don't step on any," I warned the kids. "Check the floor before you walk."

Kids were scuttling around on the floor, gathering worms. Kids were huddled in their seats, trying to avoid worms. Sammy was shrieking, "MINE! Give it back!" and the driver was glaring.

I couldn't decide whether to toss Sammy out the window or squish him first.

"Hush!" I kept hissing at him. "We're getting them all back. Hush."

Finally we had all the worms gathered, except the one on the bottom of the little girl's shoe. I didn't ask for that one back. Actually, I wasn't sure we had the rest. I just hoped we did. It was obvious the driver didn't care for worms.

Once they were all back in the bag, the driver stood up and glared at me and Sammy.

"Sammy," she said sternly. "No worms on the bus! Okay?"

Sammy burst out crying.

The driver gave me a helpless look and sat back down to finish her job, which was getting us to school.

"Ssh!" I told Sammy. "We got them all back. See?"

He just kept crying.

I put my arm around him and patted his back and shoulder, trying to settle him down. I wasn't so mad at him anymore. He did feel awfully bad about his worms. He must have really cared about them. I could understand caring about things no one else seemed to care about.

I patted and patted, and finally Sammy quieted

down. His shoulders shook now and then, and he snuffled every so often, but at least he wasn't howling.

When we got to school I handed him his bag and took his hand. He looked at me and tried to smile, his big brown eyes red and sad.

"T'ank you, buddy," he said. "Fo' finding my wums."

"You're welcome, buddy," I told him.

"I like you, buddy," Sammy said.

I just smiled. "I like you, too." I told him. But I was glad, again, that I had forgotten to bring him a treat. Worms and cookies were not a good combination.

13.
Party Pictures

As we had planned, Stacy, Andrea, Carly, and I watched the boys play football. We didn't join in, and nobody even hinted that we'd been practicing. Nobody seemed to notice that I should have been out there playing, either, which made me kind of mad. But I was going to get my team back! At my party.

After the game, there were still a few minutes of recess left, and, as usual, the boys crowded around Stacy. She laughed and talked with them for a few minutes, then slipped away, beckoning to me.

I followed her over to the bench with Andrea and Carly.

"Look," Stacy whispered, holding out her notebook.

I took it, surprised. She never lets anyone read her diary! I looked at the notebook.

I saw circles and arrows.

I looked at Stacy's excited face.

"See!" Stacy said. "Your dad showed us that play, and Mark had the offense running it." She flipped the page. "And this is as close as I could figure out . . . see, it's that play where Mark faked the handoff and then passed."

I burst out laughing. I couldn't help myself. "Stacy, you're too much!" I said, giggling. "Diagramming football plays!"

She looked offended for a minute, then giggled, too. "I even watched the game this Sunday," she admitted. "My mom thought I'd gone nuts. But it was fun. You were right, Jenelle. Now look." She pointed to the circles she'd drawn. "If there'd been someone here, blocking, this player could have made it past the guard and charged right in for the sack."

Carly suddenly started giggling, too, and then Andrea joined in.

"We HAVE gone nuts," Carly said. "Listen to you two! And look. The boys are all watching us, wondering what we're saying about them."

"They probably think we're discussing who's cute and who's cool and who we'd like to go with," Andrea said. "They'd die if they knew the truth!"

It really was funny. We kept looking at the boys and laughing. The bell rang and we went into class, but even there, all Andrea had to do was look at me and we'd start laughing again.

Then, every time we started settling down, Stacy would innocently tap her notebook and that would get us started again.

I think we'd have laughed all afternoon except for two things. One was, Ms. Kennedy kept glaring at us. That slowed us down, but didn't stop the giggles altogether.

The second thing did. I noticed that the boys were looking hurt. Like they'd decided we were laughing at them. Which we were, in a way, but not like they thought. It isn't fun to be laughed at.

I couldn't stand hurting their feelings, so when Kyle poked me and asked me what was so funny, I thought fast.

"My mom took pictures of us at a party I had this weekend," I whispered. "They are ridiculous!"

Kyle looked relieved, and I felt better until he whispered, "I want to see them. Please?"

Word spreads fast! At our afternoon recess all we heard was, "Let us see those famous pictures!" or, "When are you bringing them for show-and-tell?" or, "I'll give you five bucks for the negatives."

All I'd been trying to do was keep from hurting the boys' feelings, and I created a mess! The boys teased us all recess, imagining out loud what we were doing in the pictures. Even the other girls were asking to see them.

"I'll bet you played strip poker," José said.

"We did NOT!" Carly told him indignantly.

"Spin the toothpaste, then," Bobby guessed.

"No, we did not," Stacy said firmly.

"Ha!" Gabe said knowingly, "You didn't have to ask what those games were. That means you already know!"

"I'd give anything to see those pictures," Mark said. "Think about it, ladies. Anything in the world could be yours. All you have to do is ask. And show me a few snapshots. No big deal."

Stacy glared at him, but I knew she enjoyed his attention. "Why don't you go pick on some first-graders or something?" she asked. "That's about your mental capacity."

"Are they really that bad?" Stacy asked me when the boys were too far away to hear.

"Who?" I asked.

"The pictures!" Andrea said. "Let us see them!"

"I don't have them," I admitted. "I haven't even seen them myself. I just said we were giggling about the pictures because we were laughing so hard about the football secret, and I could tell the guys thought we were making fun of them. I didn't mean to start anything."

"You definitely started something," Carly said. "Those boys are not going to let up. We're going to be hearing about those pictures forever!"

"Are they being developed?" Andrea asked.

I nodded.

78

"Bring them as soon as you get them," Carly told me. "I'm dying to see them."

"Yeah. You and everybody else," I said.

I got the pictures Wednesday night.

Mom handed me the envelope as soon as she walked in the door. She and Dad were both grinning, so I knew they'd already peeked at the pictures.

I carried the envelope to the table, ripped it open, and pulled out the folder that was inside. It was stuffed with pictures. Bulging with pictures.

I burst out laughing when I looked at the very first one! There was Stacy, looking furious, bopping me with a pillow. There she was four times. Mom had gotten four copies of each picture, one for each of us girls.

Mom must have sneaked downstairs several times to take them because she had shots of us dancing, shots of us fighting, shots of us being goofy. She had the whole party right there on film. Four pictures each.

"How'd you do it without us noticing?" I asked.

She looked smug. "You weren't exactly paying attention to me," she said. "Besides, with the new lenses and high-speed film, low-light photography is no big deal."

She'd gotten some great close-ups with her new telephoto lens. She had Stacy looking wistful, Carly making faces, Andrea thinking. She had

Stacy drinking from the cup backwards, Stacy falling, Andrea with her foot in the popcorn bowl. She had us in our clothes, in our pajamas, and in our sleeping bags, sound asleep.

"Well, what do you think?" Mom asked. "Am I a good sneak?"

"You're a great sneak!" I told her. "The pictures are fabulous! The girls will just die when they see them. Andrea in the popcorn bowl is the best one."

"I got some pretty good ones of you, too," she said, thumbing through the stack. "Look, isn't this cute?"

Cute? I thought. There I stood in my shortie nightgown, demonstrating how to catch a football. I was cradling an imaginary ball to my chest.

"You look like you're pretending to hug someone," Mom said, grinning. "And look at this one."

I was jamming my face full of popcorn, using both hands.

"This is my favorite."

There I was, hands propped under my chin, thinking. I remembered what I had been thinking about, and I could feel my face turning red.

"You look like you're dreaming about Prince Charming," Mom told me, "It's a wonderful shot. I'm better than I thought. Of course, I had great subjects to work with."

"Prince Charming!" I snorted, returning the pictures to the stack. "I was feeling sad because

I realized I can never be a pro football player." I didn't mention that I was also thinking about kissing — some day.

Mom laughed. "That's my Jenelle," she said, rumpling my hair.

14.
An Even Number of Boys and Girls

Thursday morning I double-checked my back-pack. I had separated the pictures into sets and put three sets in envelopes marked Carly, Andrea, and Stacy. I left mine home.

Sammy had on his fuzzy blue coat again because it was a chilly morning, but it wasn't zipped and he wasn't wearing the hat or mittens. He ran over and gave me a hug.

"Here, Sammy," his mother called, rattling a paper bag. "Don't forget your camera. He's going to take pictures of his friends at school," she said to me. "And, Jenelle, I'm sorry about the worms. I thought he had some little trucks in the bag."

"So did I," I told her. We grinned at each other.

At school, I handed Sammy off to his teacher and left to find my own friends. I waited by the playground, beckoning to the girls as they passed by. We huddled in a group, standing in a pile of silvery-green leaves that crackled underfoot as I reached into my pack and pulled out the envelopes.

I handed them around, and watched while the girls examined the pictures. My smile grew broader as their faces got redder.

"I can't believe this!" Andrea said. "How did she get so many pictures without us knowing it?"

"High-speed film and a new telephoto lens," I said. "She got it for her birthday."

"Look at me!" Stacy said, showing a picture around. "In my shortie nightie! I'm practically indecent!"

"Look!" Carly said. "Andrea in the bowl. This is great!"

"I would DIE if the boys saw these!" Andrea said, giggling. "They're great, but I'd die if anyone saw them. Look at me! I'm drenched from Stacy's water."

"At least you're not looking like an idiot with your chin in a glass of water," Stacy said. "I look like an idiot!"

Andrea tapped the picture that showed her with her foot in the bowl. "THIS is an idiot," she said. "This one is the most idiotic of all."

"You look like you're in love, Jenelle," Carly said, holding up the photo of me thinking.

"Yeah, you do," the others agreed. "It's a beautiful picture."

83

"Well, keep it beautifully hidden!" I said. "Come on. It's time to go in."

I was nervous all day. I was afraid the boys would get a hold of the pictures somehow. I was even afraid one of the girls would accidently-on-purpose let the news out that we had them.

I was sure the boys would figure it out anyway, because Andrea and Stacy were giggling overtime all day. Every time someone mentioned the pictures to tease us about them, Stacy would gasp or look secretive and giggle. Andrea wasn't much better. Carly kept catching my eye and looking at me poker-faced, but at least we didn't break into hysterics like the other two did.

Ms. Kennedy finally got disgusted, I guess, because she piled on the homework.

"If you can't do your work IN class, you'll just have to do it at home," she said.

She gave us a ton of homework. "I want the answers to the Chapter Check-up tomorrow," she said. "And by Monday I want you to have read the whole next chapter. Tuesday you'll have a test on both chapters."

Tuesday! I thought, horrified. On two chapters! That isn't enough time!

It was even less time than I thought it would be because Stacy couldn't quit calling all weekend. Her cousin was getting married, and Stacy was going to be the flower girl. She wanted to talk about weddings and lace and dresses — all the things that she knows I think are dumb. I listened politely as long as I could stand it, but when Stacy started planning the dresses for her own wedding, I figured that was enough!

"Your wedding won't be for at least ten years!" I told her. "Do you think maybe we could wait eight more years before we plan the clothes?"

Stacy groaned at me. "You have no sense of romance at all," she said. "Planning a wedding takes a lot of time and thought."

"When I get married, everyone will have to wear NFL T-shirts," I said. "That doesn't require any thought at all. See? My wedding's planned. And I need to go help with dinner. My parents have company coming over, and Mom's been knocking herself out making a fancy feast."

Stacy giggled. "You make it sound like cat food," she said.

"It smells better than that," I said.

"There's one more thing," Stacy said. "I've been going over my party invitations, and Jenelle, there's nobody to invite for you."

"What do you mean?" I asked. "This isn't a dating party, Stacy. You've invited lots of boys I like."

"I know you like them, but will you dance with them?"

"I don't know," I said.

"This is a dancing party," Stacy said. "I want everyone to dance!"

"I'll dance with everyone who asks me," I promised. "And if no one asks me it's no big deal."

"It is, too," she said gloomily. "You think about it, okay? You can ask anyone you like. There needs to be an even number of boys and girls. You can't be the only one there without a partner. Please?"

"Sure," I said. "I'll think about it. I've really got to go help. 'Bye."

Maybe I should just stay home, I thought, heading for the kitchen. Then there WOULD be an even number of boys and girls!

15.
Sammy Strikes Again

I wasn't really ready for the test Tuesday, but I had managed to study my English a little after the Sunday games, before Monday night football, and in between calls from Stacy.

Sammy was bouncing with excitement when I picked him up. He bounced across the street holding my hand, bounced up the bus steps, and bounced into our seat.

"I got my pictahs!" he crowed.

I remembered he'd taken his camera for show-and-tell, to take pictures of his friends, but I still flinched when he reached inside his paper bag. I was half expecting him to bring out a handful of worms, but all he pulled out was an envelope full of pictures.

The kid had talent! His pictures were really good, and all he'd used was a little pocket camera. I'd expected a few blurry shots and pictures taken from too far away to tell what was in them.

But he had twenty-four great pictures. They were all centered, all closeups, all perfectly exposed. Not one was blurry. Some of the kids were making faces, but they were still good shots.

"Sammy, these are great!" I told him. "How come you're so good at taking pictures?"

Sammy wiggled with pride. "My brothah taught me," he said.

"That's right, your mom said something about a brother," I said. "He must ride the early bus." That would mean he was in junior high. He couldn't ride our bus or he'd be Sammy's bus buddy. And I'd know him.

But Sammy shook his head. "Daddy takes him," he said. "To practice. Only he's not my brothah's daddy."

I let that one pass. A lot of kids have dads who aren't their dads, and brothers who aren't their brothers. If Sammy's parents had been divorced and remarried, or if Sammy's brother was adopted or a foster child, it wasn't my business. I just listened to Sammy chatter and enjoyed the bus ride without worms.

The only mishap we had was my fault. I'd propped my backpack next to me, which meant next to the aisle, and when we went around the sharp curve that's near the school, Sammy leaned against me. I was being silly, so I leaned sideways to make him tip more, and my pack dumped into the aisle.

Pencils went rolling and books flying. I'd forgotten to zip it shut.

"Sammy pick them up!" he offered, and scurried around me, kneeling down in the aisle to gather my things.

How sweet! I thought.

As we parked at the school, he handed me my pack.

"Thanks!" I told him. "Now, have you got everything? Your pictures?"

He nodded, his brown eyes solemn. He patted his paper bag.

"Let's go, then." I handed him off to his teacher and went to find Stacy and the crew.

At lunch recess I found Stacy, Andrea, and Carly standing by the maple tree on the edge of the playground.

"What's going on?" I asked. "Where are the boys?" If Stacy was in a group, there were usually boys standing near, too.

Stacy shrugged. "I don't know, and I don't care," she said.

"Why?" I asked. "What's wrong? You look mad."

She shrugged again.

"Honest, Jenelle," Carly said. "Where have you been? You're a space case these days, I swear."

"What are you talking about?" I asked, looking at my friends. They all looked mad at something. "What's going on?"

"You didn't notice the boys laughing at us all morning?" Andrea asked.

"All the smart-aleck looks and the snickering?" Carly added.

I thought back. The class had been pretty rowdy this morning, even during our test. Ms. Kennedy had threatened to give us all Fs if we didn't settle down, but I hadn't realized it was the boys causing all the problems.

"I guess so," I said. "What were they laughing at?"

"No one knows," Stacy told me. "But they're giggling and smirking and pointing at us, and I'm so mad I'm ready to cancel my party. I would, too, except I'm too excited about it. It's only three more days, not counting Saturday. But those boys are really being obnoxious!"

"Maybe they'll be back to normal by Saturday," I said. "Maybe there's some joke going around, and it'll die out by then."

"Look, there they are," Andrea said.

The boys were all clustered in a group, their backs to us. They were looking at something, and laughing so hard we could hear them clear across the playground.

"I wish I knew what was so funny," Carly muttered.

"I'll go ask," I said.

But when I got close to the cluster of boys they poked each other, quickly hiding whatever they were looking at. They looked guilty.

"How's it going?" Mark asked, too quickly, and too innocently.

Bobby smirked, and Jason elbowed him. They both tried to look like nothing had happened.

"What so funny?" I asked.

"Nothing," Mark said. "Honest."

They looked like they were about to explode laughing, but they wouldn't explain why. Disgusted, I trudged back to the girls.

"They won't tell me," I said.

They kept it up all day long, and all day Wednesday. They were having so much fun teasing us and being obnoxious that they didn't bother to play football at all. That meant I didn't have to watch my replacement quarterback, and it meant I wasn't missing any action because there wasn't any. But that didn't make me feel any better.

Stacy called me every night to see if I'd figured anything out, and by Wednesday night she was nearly in tears. "I don't like Mark anymore," she said. "I don't even know if I want to have my party. I was worried about you not having anyone to dance with, but it looks like I'm the one who won't have anyone!"

"You can't be serious," I said. "Even by your standards, it isn't time for this romance to end."

"It never was a romance," Stacy said glumly.

"You got all dreamy-eyed," I reminded her. "Just thinking of him made you act silly. That's a romance."

"You just don't understand," Stacy said. "It has to go both ways to be a romance. I don't think he was all that interested in me, and right now, I'm glad! Because I hate him! All the guys are being rats, but he's the main rat."

"You'll get over it, Stace," I promised.

"No, I won't," she said. "He's an obnoxious rat."

"So you won't care if I don't invite him to my party?" I asked hopefully.

"I'm not sure I'm inviting him to mine," she said.

"You already did," I reminded her. "Are you going to cancel the invitation?"

"I guess not," she said, sighing. "It would be rude to do that. And even if I don't like him, I don't want to be rude."

"Are you going to cancel your party then?" I asked. "You could probably do that without being rude. Just think up some excuse."

Stacy sighed again. Then she giggled.

"I just remembered something," she said. "Remember that dinner I went to? To meet the family of the guy my cousin's marrying?"

"Yeah?" I asked. "What does that have to do with your party?"

"Remember that cute guy I told you about who was there? Christopher?"

"I think so," I said. I didn't really remember because I hadn't really been listening. Stacy had described every guy in detail, and after two or three descriptions I'd just tuned her out.

"Well, my cousin said he asked about me," Stacy said, giggling again.

"So?"

"Jenelle, you are totally dense!" Stacy said. "If he asked about me, that means he was interested. I was interested, or at least I would have been if I'd known I was going to hate Mark by now."

"I think I got it," I said. "You're going to invite Christopher to your party. So you're not going to cancel it."

"Right. And we won't have an uneven number of girls and boys, either. And I won't have to dance with Mark, or any of those other hopeless guys."

Stacy sounded triumphant. I felt discouraged. Not only was I not getting out of the dancing party, and not only did I have to leave my football home, but I would have to be at a dancing party without a football WITH all the the mysteriously secretive guys from our class.

By Thursday morning I'd decided I was going to have the mystery explained or I was going to start knocking heads. It takes a lot to get me mad, but once I'm there, I'm definitely mad! The boys were being so obnoxious they were unbearable!

I was so mad, I just nodded at Mrs. Grundy, took Sammy's hand, and marched us across to the bus. I didn't even realize Sammy was talking to me until I finally noticed his little tugs on my jacket sleeve.

"What?" I asked, trying to sound patient. After all, I wasn't mad at him.

"Can I have my pictahs?" he asked, looking solemn.

"Sammy, I don't have your pictures," I told him. "Remember, you had them in a paper bag?"

He shook his head. "Have yo' pictahs in the bag," he said.

"Huh?" I asked, thoroughly confused.

"Yo' stuff fall down," Sammy said. " 'Member?"

"Right," I told him. "My pack fell, and you helped pick everything up. That was very nice of you."

"Yo' pictahs fall out," he said. "And when I pick yo' pictahs up, mine fall out, too. I goof, buddy. I put my pictahs in your foldah 'stead of yo's. I put yo' pictahs in my bag."

"But I didn't have any pictures . . ." I started to say. Then I got a horrified feeling. I remembered looking at my party pictures while I was studying for my test, and I didn't remember seeing my pictures after that, or looking in my folder. Once I was finished studying, I didn't need

94

the review folder till the next test. I yanked my pack open and snatched out the folder.

There was a picture envelope inside. My hands shook as I opened the envelope.

"Oh, no!" I moaned. They were Sammy's pictures, not mine.

"My pictahs!" he said, delighted. "T'ank you, buddy!"

"Sammy," I said carefully. "What happened to my pictures?"

"I gave them to a big boy on the playground," he said cheerfully. "I tol' him to give them to my buddy!"

Suddenly everything was all too clear!

16.
I Hate Boys!

"So that's the story," I said glumly.

Stacy, Carly, and Andrea all looked sick.

"The boys have the pictures," Andrea said, her face bleak. "All of them."

"We're all in our shortie nighties," Carly reminded us, as if we could have forgotten.

"I'll kill them," Stacy vowed. "I'll strangle them one at a time."

"We have to get the pictures back before you kill them," I told her. "They've got the negatives, too. They were all in the envelope together."

"I'd like to strangle Sammy, too," Stacy said.

"He's too cute to strangle," I said. "Besides, it wasn't his fault. It was mine. Strangle me."

"How are we going to get them back?" Andrea asked.

"The boys are not going to hand them over just because we ask them to," Carly added.

"They know perfectly well those pictures don't belong to them," Andrea said. "And they know perfectly well who they do belong to. They are rotten. Every one of those boys is stinking rotten. I hate boys!"

"I don't want to have my party now," Stacy said sadly. "Even though I invited Christopher and he's coming. I'd hate to miss seeing him again, but how can I face those rats? I'm not sure I could stand dancing with Christopher in the same room with those guys! I don't even want to look at them. Ever again!" She looked like she was going to cry.

"We've got to get something on them," I said, thinking. "We've got to make them so eager to give those pictures back they'll be standing in line to hand them over."

"But how?" Carly asked.

"I think I may have just figured it out," I said slowly, grinning as an idea came to me. "I've got it. Have I ever got it! Listen . . ."

I started whispering, outlining my plan. As I explained, the girls' faces looked less and less glum. They started smiling, then laughing.

"It's a fabulous idea!" Stacy said, giggling.

"An inspiration!" Carly said.

"I'll make the list," Stacy volunteered. "I'll give you each your assignment before we leave this afternoon."

"Do you want me to write down what to say?" I asked.

"Yes, please," Carly said.

"Okay," I said, feeling pretty smug.

"You are brilliant!" Stacy told me.

I nodded. "I know," I said.

We drove the boys crazy all day Thursday. We stood in a group at lunch, laughing at them, like they'd laughed at us the last two days. We smirked and grinned and pointed. They looked uncertain. They couldn't figure out what we had to laugh about.

Every few minutes one of us would think about my plan and burst out laughing again, and the boys looked more confused each time. They tried to laugh back at us, but their hearts weren't in it. They started whispering to each other.

"I know what they're saying," I told my friends. "They've decided maybe we don't know they have the pictures after all. They can't figure out why we're not upset. I'll bet you anything one of them will come over here and tell us they have them, just to make sure we know we should be mad and embarrassed."

Sure enough, in a minute, Bobby came sauntering over, trying to look casual.

"Nice day, girls," he said.

We nodded.

The other boys came wandering over, too. They couldn't stand missing the fun.

"Lose anything?" Bobby asked.

Carly and I looked at each other in innocent

surprise. I looked at the other girls.

"Are we missing anything?" I asked.

Stacy shrugged. "Nothing important," she said.

"Like maybe . . . these?" Bobby held up a handful of pictures, out of our reach, of course.

I glanced at his hand like he was holding nothing more interesting than a hair ribbon.

"Oh, those," I said, yawning. "Like I said, nothing important."

Bobby looked astounded. The other boys looked confused.

The bell rang, signaling the end of recess, and the boys walked off looking puzzled and very disappointed.

Stacy, Carly, Andrea, and I looked at each other and burst out laughing.

"This is too good!" Andrea said. "They can't stand it!"

"They expected us to scream and try to grab the pictures," Carly said, smothering her giggles with her hands. "They don't know what to do now. We aren't reacting properly!"

"By Saturday night we'll have them so confused they won't know if they're coming or going," Stacy said.

"And then we'll whammy them again!" Carly said. "I love it!"

"Let's go," I told them. "Only one hour of school left today. And then one more day of school before Stacy's party."

"Let's really lay it on," Stacy said. "We can drive them totally crazy by tomorrow afternoon! They won't even be able to enjoy trick-or-treating when we get done with them. They'll be sorry they ever even thought about looking at our pictures!"

17.
Halloween

By Friday afternoon the guys were totally perplexed — definitely off guard, but definitely still planning to go to Stacy's party. We'd made sure of that. I went home happy with a good day's work and ready to have a great time trick-or-treating.

We haven't had any problems in our town with poisoned candy scares, but Mom reviewed all the safety rules with me anyway. I promised to use my flashlight at all times, stay in the neighborhoods I knew, cross the streets only at corners, and save all my candy until I had checked it out at home.

Mom handed me the reflective tape she'd saved for me to put on Sammy's back and I headed off. I had tape on my jacket, too. Sammy and I would be highly visible.

"You're the grown-up tonight, you know," Mom

told me. "Trick-or-treating will be a little different when you have to be responsible for a little one."

"I'll be fine, Mom," I said. Trick-or-treating is trick-or-treating, I thought. Sammy isn't going to make it any different.

I'd borrowed football pads from the P.E. teacher and a helmet from a kid up the street. With white stretch pants, an NFL T-shirt, and smears of black paint on my cheekbones, I made a terrific football player.

Sammy was all dressed up, waiting for me. He was a spidery kind of bug — a perfect costume for Sammy! He had on black furry leggings and a black furry hat with little antennae sticking up. He wore a black leotard with orange stripes and had big orange crepe paper bows on his shoes. I couldn't think of any bugs that had orange bows on their feet, but Sammy was adorable, anyway.

Mrs. Grundy reviewed the safety rules with me, too.

"Sammy can stay out till seven-thirty if he lasts that long," she told me. "Here's a key. His brother's at a party, and I don't expect him back until late, so you'll need the key to get back in. The plane's due in at six forty-five so I'll probably be back around eight, depending on how long we have to wait for the luggage. I'll call if there's any delay. Do you have any questions?"

I shook my head. "I think I've got it," I said. I

used the reflective tape to put an X on the back of Sammy's cape, which he was struggling to put on.

"Oh, what a good idea!" Mrs. Grundy said, helping him. "I'll remember the tape for next year."

Sammy looked even more adorable in his fuzzy black cape. It hung down almost to his ankles and looked plenty warm.

His mother locked the door behind us, and gave Sammy a kiss. "Now, mind Jenelle," she told him. "She's the boss tonight, right?"

"Right," Sammy agreed, his eyes huge and solemn as he clutched his candy bag.

"Oh, I almost forgot," Mrs. Grundy said. "Here's a few pieces of candy for him to nibble on in case he has trouble waiting."

I stuffed the candy in my pocket, and we waved good-bye while we headed next door.

It was just getting dark. Not many kids were out yet, except a few smaller ones with parents. They were up the street a ways.

"Now you knock," I told Sammy.

He shook his head, his eyes growing larger and darker.

"I scared," he said.

"There's nothing to be scared of," I told him. "We knock on the door, and when the people open it we say, 'Trick or treat!' and then they put candy in our bags."

His eyes lit up. "Tanny?" he said eagerly.

"Yes. Or pennies or balloons or a pencil," I added. "A treat of some kind."

"Tanny," he said firmly.

"Now knock," I said.

He shook his head.

"Okay. I'll knock."

The woman who answered the door smiled at us. "Hi, Sammy," she said. "Are you trick-or-treating?"

Sammy nodded.

"Then say, 'Trick or treat,' " she suggested.

Sammy shook his head.

"I guess he's shy," I told her. I said it for both of us to show Sammy how to do it, and the woman put a small Snickers candy bar in my bag.

"Hold your bag out, Sammy," she told him.

He shook his head.

"I can't put any candy in it if you don't hold it out where I can reach it," she explained.

Sammy thought about that. I could see his struggle on his face. He was afraid to hold the bag out, but he did want that candy!

Greed finally won. He held the bag out about two inches from his body, and the woman was able to drop the candy inside.

"T'anks!" Sammy said, smiling widely.

We went to the next house. Sammy still wouldn't knock or say 'Trick or treat,' but he did hold the bag out for the roll of Lifesavers. And he did say, "T'anks!"

At the fifth house we were joined by other kids in costume. Sammy took one look at them and let out a shriek.

"Monsters!" he screamed, grabbing my leg. "Gonna eat me!"

"No, no," I assured him, patting his fuzzy back. "They're just kids. Just like you." I bent down, pried him loose from my leg, and put my hands on his shoulders, my bag dangling behind him.

"Look," I said, tapping his cape. "This is Sammy. Sammy is wearing funny clothes to look like a bug."

"Spidah," he corrected me.

"Right, a spider," I said. "You look like a spider, but you're really Sammy. Those kids are just kids, too. They're wearing funny clothes, just like you are."

Sammy shook his head. "Monster," he said. "Ghost. Not spidah."

"Right," I told him, sighing. "They aren't spiders like you are, but they're kids, just like you are. People dress up in funny clothes on Halloween. That's what it's for. We all wear costumes."

Sammy looked doubtful, but by then the kids were up the street from us, so he took my hand again and waited for me to knock.

Every time we passed another group of kids,

Sammy would shiver and hide his head against my side. I wondered if I should take him home, but he calmed down as soon as the kids left. I decided to keep going.

By the time we reached the end of the block it was fully dark. It was taking a long time to get anywhere with all the pauses while people went by us. I held the flashlight and my bag in one hand and Sammy clutched my other hand as tightly as he could. He liked being given candy, but I was really beginning to think he was too young and frightened to be out trick-or-treating. He was a lot of trouble. Mom may have been right after all!

Finally I asked him if he wanted to go home.

He shook his head. "Tanny," he said firmly, rattling his bag.

"Okay," I agreed. "I'd like a little more loot myself."

"We trudged up the next walk, and I rang the doorbell.

The door opened.

Sammy screamed, dropped his bag, and grabbed both of my legs with both of his hands.

"I'm sorry!" The man who had opened the door took off his vampire mask. "I didn't mean to scare him. It's Sammy, isn't it?"

I nodded.

"Sammy," he said, "Sammy, it's just me. It's Mr. Evans. Billy's daddy. I didn't mean to scare you, Sammy!"

Sammy finally quit crying and shuddering and took a quick look, hiding his face again immediately. He let what he had seen during his quick peek settle in his mind for a minute, then looked again.

"Hi, Mister Ebban!" he said cheerfully. He retrieved his bag and held it out. "Got tanny?"

Mr. Evans laughed and shook his head. "Fast recuperation!" he said. "Amazing what a little candy will do, huh?"

He gave us both a whole handful of suckers, smiled at Sammy's "T'anks!" and closed the door.

"Are you sure you don't want to go home?" I asked him. "You keep getting scared."

Sammy shook his head. "Tanny!" he said.

So on we went. We developed a routine after the scare Sammy had at Mr. Evans' house. We would stand in front of the door. Sammy would hide his face against my leg. If a normal person answered the door, I'd whisper, "Okay, Sammy," and he would look up. If someone in costume answered, I'd explain that Sammy was afraid of costumes, and I'd help him hold out his bag without looking.

It was not how I thought I'd be spending Halloween night, but in a way, it was even more fun. I felt grown-up and responsible and I still got plenty of loot.

I'd planned a route out for us, but with all the time Sammy spent hiding his face, I could tell we'd be lucky to get half of it covered by seven-thirty.

The third block from his house was a wonderful surprise. The whole block was decked out for Halloween! Every house that I could see from the corner had bright lights or spooky music, or dummies or ghosts dangling from trees. It looked great!

"They must be having a block party!" I said. "Let's go! They'll have great treats on this block! These are obviously Halloween people!"

I started for the first house, dragging Sammy. He dug in his heels.

"No!" he shrieked. "I scared!"

"I want to trick-or-treat on this block, Sammy," I told him. "See how fun it looks? I've already explained there's nothing to be scared of. Now, come on. Let's go."

He shook his head, shivering in his fuzzy cape. "Monsters," he said. "Eat me! I scared."

"Then I'll carry you," I said. "I think this block looks great." I picked him up and started off. I wasn't grown-up and responsible enough to let one tired little boy ruin my fun.

I was right. It was a block party, with bunches of costumed people moving from house to house, calling to each other. The people who were handing out treats were giving apples, oranges, popcorn balls, pencils, and full-sized candy bars. We also got a quarter and a box of animal crackers.

Sammy hid his face and ignored it all. I held his bag out for him.

When we got to the house with the spooky music he clutched me tighter. He was getting awfully heavy.

"Can you walk a while?" I asked.

He didn't answer, but I could tell he was shaking his head no. We got cartoon erasers there. I made it to two more houses before my arms gave out.

"I have to put you down," I said. "You're too heavy. You have to walk." I checked my watch. "It's almost time to go home, anyway," I added.

"No!" Sammy yelled. "I wanna twitter-tweat!"

"Then let's do it!" I said firmly.

Sammy looked around, wide-eyed. He didn't seem able to figure a way he could refuse to trick-or-treat, and still trick-or-treat at the same time.

He marched with me up the next set of steps. He shivered a little at the fierce faces on the jack-o'-lanterns. I knocked. He hid his face until I whispered, "Okay," then held his bag out.

The man who answered my knock was in costume, but since he was in a cowboy costume I didn't think Sammy would be afraid.

"Trick or treat," I told him.

"What's the trick?" he asked.

"What?" I said.

"You do a trick for me, and I give you a treat," he said. "Isn't that how it goes?"

"What's the treat?" I asked. "I have to decide if it's worth it."

He grinned and held up a packet of flower seeds.

"No!" Sammy said loudly. "Tanny!"

"Ssh!" I told him. I didn't want the guy to be embarrassed that Sammy didn't want his treat, which meant I felt obligated to think up a trick to do. I'd have preferred a large candy bar, but flower seeds wasn't a bad idea.

"Is your refrigerator running?" I asked the guy.

"That's an old joke," he said. "Not good enough."

"Tanny!" Sammy yelled.

"What is he saying?" the man asked.

"He wants candy," I explained. "That's okay. He has enough candy already. I think the flower seeds are a fine idea. I'll think of a trick in a minute."

"Sammy want tanny!" Sammy screamed. Then he threw himself down on the porch, kicking his feet and screaming as loudly as he could.

I was so embarrassed I could have died. I bent down, swooped Sammy up into my arms, and stuffed a piece of the candy his mother had given me into his mouth. He quit screeching and sucked happily on the Starburst.

"That's the best trick I've seen tonight!" the man said, smiling at me. "Here's your seeds, and

110

his, too. He doesn't want them. Here, take an extra package. I have a feeling you're going to have to cut your night short and get him home to bed!"

"I'm afraid you're right," I agreed sadly. As great as this block was, I was going to have to skip the rest of it. Sammy just couldn't handle any more.

"Good night, and happy Halloween," the man said as he closed his door. "Great trick, young lady. You have talent. Definite talent!"

18.
The Black Ninja

I didn't even bother trying to trick-or-treat on the way home. Sammy was so tired he could barely stumble along, and I could only carry him for a few minutes before I had to put him down again.

He was too tired to notice the kids in costumes, so at least I didn't have to keep stopping for him to hide his face. My arms felt like logs by the time I finally dumped Sammy on his own porch.

I dug out the key and let us in. Mrs. Grundy had left the lights on for us and a package of hot dogs in the fridge in case we were hungry. She'd also told me I could make hot chocolate while I was waiting for her.

Sammy didn't want hot chocolate. He didn't want food. He climbed up on the couch in his costume and sat, looking wide-eyed around the room, like he wasn't sure where he was.

I helped him get his hat and cape off, but when I tried to take off his shoes he shook his head. He blinked, then his eyes fluttered shut, and he slowly toppled over onto the couch.

I slid his shoes off, covered him up with his cape, and propped his bag of candy next to him. Then I made myself a hot dog and some hot chocolate.

I was mostly responsible tonight, I decided, even if I did get candy. Stacy thought it was too juvenile to dress up for Halloween so she stayed home and gave out candy. But I think I had acted pretty grown-up . . . in my own way.

I waited for Mrs. Grundy to come home, answering the door for a few trick-or-treaters who came by. I called my mom to tell her that Sammy's parents weren't back yet, but that I expected them any minute.

At eight o'clock Mrs. Grundy called.

"I'm still waiting for the plane," she said. "It was delayed but it's supposed to be in pretty soon. How's everything going?"

"Fine," I told her. "Sammy's asleep on the couch. Do you want me to put him to bed?"

"No, he's too heavy for you to carry around. He'll be fine where he is until we get home. Can you stay longer? Will your parents let you?"

"I called them," I said. "They said I could stay till you got home."

"Thanks, Jenelle," she said. "We'll give you a ride home when we get there. You shouldn't walk home alone this time of night. Did Sammy have fun?"

"Mostly," I told her. "He got scared a few times, but he mostly had fun."

"Well, thanks again," she said. "I'm certainly glad Sammy didn't have to spend Halloween here at the airport! I'll call again if there's another delay. Otherwise, expect me about nine o'clock."

I called my parents back, and Mom sounded relieved that I'd be getting a ride home.

"I can't believe this!" I told her. "I just wandered around for two hours in the dark, taking care of a little kid, and now you're nervous about me walking four blocks home?"

"It's later now," Mom said, as if that explained everything. "You accept the ride, okay?"

"Okay."

No more trick-or-treaters came to Sammy's house, and I hadn't brought a book to read since I hadn't expected to be stuck here. I wandered into the living room, glancing out the window every time I saw headlights. I debated whether to turn on the TV, but I didn't really feel like staring at it, so I left it off.

Suddenly I froze.

The front door was opening! I hadn't locked it after Sammy and I got home. No one had driven up, so it couldn't be Sammy's folks. I didn't know what to do!

The door swung open.

I took a deep breath, getting ready to scream.

A figure dressed in a black Ninja outfit slipped through the door, spun, and whipped off his black hood.

The figure stood there staring at me.

It took me a second to recognize him.

It was Mark.

19.
Hot Chocolate

"Mark!" I said, very glad I hadn't screamed. I would have died of embarrassment if I'd screamed! "What are you doing here?"

"You're the baby-sitter?" he asked, closing the door behind him. "You're Sammy's bus buddy?"

I nodded. "So, who are you?" I asked. "You can't be . . ."

"I'm Sammy's brother," he said. "Or half-brother, actually."

"Then why aren't you his bus buddy?" I asked. "Why aren't you on the bus?"

"I moved here after they started the buddy program," he reminded me. "Besides, I go to practice in the mornings. And I work in the afternoons."

I remembered Sammy telling me his father, but not his brother's father, took his brother to practice in the morning. "What do you practice?" I asked.

116

"Football," he said. "I told Mom I wouldn't move here unless she found me a league to join. She found one at the Y. And that worked out well because they hired me to help coach the little kids after school. Where is Mom? I thought she'd be home by now."

I explained about the delayed plane.

"Did you leave me any hot chocolate?" he asked. "Do you want me to make you some?"

I nodded. "Sure," I said. "Sounds good."

I followed him into the kitchen.

"How was the little spider tonight?" he asked, putting water in the microwave to boil. He spooned the cocoa mix into two cups.

"Not too bad," I said. "He kept getting scared, but he had fun."

"He never quits talking about you, you know," he said. When the water started boiling he poured it into the cups and stirred. "He really likes his buddy. If I'd known you were his buddy I'd have listened a little better. He's certainly a talker!"

"He's cute," I told him. "And except for the worms, it's fun watching him on the bus."

"Oh, yes, the worms!" Mark said, laughing as he handed me my cup. "I guess the bus driver talked to Sammy's teacher, and she called Mom. Sammy couldn't understand what he'd done wrong. He likes worms, so everybody should. It really was pretty funny."

"It was," I agreed. I kept noticing how happy

his whole face looked when he smiled. And how impish. He looked like he'd played plenty of worm tricks in his time.

We sat at the table in the kitchen, waiting for the chocolate to cool. "We're all kind of like that, I guess," I said. "Thinking everyone should be excited about the same things we are, should like the same things we do. Like Stacy's party."

Mark nodded thoughtfully. "It's a three-year-old's view of life. It's cute on a little kid. It's not always so cute on us older folks. Does that mean you're not excited about the party?"

I shrugged. "I'm not really into that boy-girl dancing stuff," I said.

"I like to dance," Mark said. "Will you dance with me tomorrow?"

"Sure," I told him, feeling guilty about the trick we were going to play on the guys, including him, tomorrow night.

"You look good as a football player," he said, eyeing me.

I could feel myself turning red. I'd taken my helmet off, and had forgotten that I was still in my football costume, complete with black paint smears on my face. I started dabbing my cheeks with a napkin.

"Leave it on," he said. "It looks cool. Why did you choose to be a football player for Halloween?"

I kept staring at him, and then getting embarrassed about staring, so I'd look away. Then I'd look back again. He was cute, and it seemed odd to me that I was noticing that. I wasn't sure what was going on, but I didn't feel as easy disliking him as I did at school. In fact, I didn't dislike him at all. And that made me feel uncomfortable. I guess noticing that someone is good-looking makes a difference in how you feel around them.

"You don't know, or you don't want to tell me?" he asked.

"Know what?" I asked, but then I remembered that he'd asked me a question. I looked at him like he was crazy. Everyone knew without asking what I'd be for Halloween! I was always a football player.

"Why did you — " He started to repeat the question.

"You don't know, do you?" I interrupted, astounded as I realized it was true. I'd been disliking him all this time because he'd taken my position at quarterback, and he didn't even know that he'd replaced me. No one had told him.

We both looked out the window at the same time, realizing that a car was pulling in. His parents were back.

"I'll walk you home," Mark offered.

Mom had said I had to accept the ride from his parents, but I really wanted to walk with Mark. I needed to apologize. And besides, I'd enjoyed his company. He was fun to be around and easy to talk to.

"Sounds great," I said. "Let me call my parents and tell them I'm on my way."

Mark went out to greet his parents, so I could make my call privately. Mom was doubtful.

"I'd feel better if you had a ride," she said.

"But I'll have company," I said. "And it's only four blocks, and I've been out all night, anyway. And besides, Mr. Grundy just got back from a business trip, and Mrs. Grundy's been at the airport all this time. I'm sure they'd be glad to stay home. I'd really like to walk. Please?"

"Oh, all right," Mom agreed. "Only come straight home, okay?"

"Right," I promised.

Mark explained that he was walking me home. Mrs. Grundy looked as doubtful as my mom had sounded.

"I got permission," I told her.

"And I was going to be walking home from the party around ten, anyway," Mark pointed out. "So I'll be fine coming back alone."

They finally agreed, and Mark and I set off, walking next to each other.

"I love Halloween," I said. "It's so spooky and fun. Did you see the block where the party was?"

"Yeah. That was great! Did you see the dummy with the bloody knife sticking out of his chest?"

"No," I said, disappointed. "I had to quit halfway through the block and take Sammy home." I told him about the screaming trick Sammy had pulled.

"He can be pretty impressive when he gets wound up," Mark commented.

"You can say that again!" I said.

Mark reached out and took my hand. My stomach jumped at his touch. It felt funny, holding a boy's hand, but very nice.

We walked on, swinging our hands together.

Mark stopped under a streetlight, looking at me. His face was serious for a minute, then he grinned at me. I didn't know why he was smiling, but I smiled back. He certainly had a nice smile!

I took a deep breath and let it out. "I have something to apologize for," I told him. "I didn't like you before tonight. At all!" I explained about being the quarterback for four years until he showed up, and how angry it had made me that none of the guys seemed to care that I wasn't involved in the games anymore.

"I'm sorry," he said quietly. "I didn't know. I'm sorry about taking your pictures, too. That was mean."

I laughed. "You're going to pay for it," I said. But I wouldn't explain. It wouldn't be fair to let him get himself out of trouble with the girls just because he was a pretty nice guy after all.

"I guess if I'm guilty, I deserve to pay," he said. We started walking again, still holding hands.

"I'm looking forward to tomorrow night," Mark said.

"Me, too," I said. I wasn't even sure I wanted to go, before, and now I was actually looking forward to it!

I felt an odd flutter of excitement inside, and I suddenly understood some of the things that had confused me, like the way Stacy had behaved when she saw Mark the first time. Not that I was ever planning to act like that, but it did make more sense!

I hoped she meant what she had said about not liking Mark any more! Otherwise things could get very unpleasant! But she'd invited Christopher. I took that as a good sign.

"Oh," I said, suddenly remembering I was having a party, too.

"A football party?" he asked, laughing, after I'd explained.

"Yeah," I said. "I got the idea to tease Stacy, because she hated football. I thought it would make her change her mind about having a dancing party." And to get my team back, I added silently. But I think that's going to work out fine, now.

"You don't like to dance?" Mark sounded disappointed. "You said you'd dance with me tomorrow."

"I will," I told him. "But when we planned the parties, Stacy couldn't play football and I couldn't dance. We taught each other."

"Won't inviting an extra person mess up your teams?"

I started laughing.

"Can you explain the joke?" Mark asked. "I missed it."

"I didn't plan the teams at all!" I admitted, shaking my head at myself. "I don't know what I was thinking about! I invited three girls, and the nine boys I play football with at recess. I can't believe how dumb I am! With me, that's thirteen people. That's not enough for two teams, at least not if we want to get a decent game going. And I do want a decent game!"

"I guess I have to come," Mark said. "Your teams are uneven. That's not good for the game, and not good for dancing. Or were you planning to dance at your party?"

"I think I am now," I told him. "And I think I'd better invite some more girls. I guess it doesn't matter whether they know how to play football or not. The idea is to have fun."

Four blocks never seemed so short to me before. I told Mark I'd see him tomorrow and went into my house, smiling. I was definitely looking forward to tomorrow night!

Stacy's party is a good idea after all, I decided. And I won't have to be giggly to enjoy it!

20.
Party Pooper

Saturday afternoon, according to plan, I made my phone calls and then hopped on my bike. After making my three stops I hurried home to shower and get ready for Stacy's party.

It was a lot more fun getting ready than I'd thought it would be. I used the blow dryer on my hair and then had Mom help me curl it. I almost put some ribbons in it, but decided I couldn't go that far!

I dug out the skirt and blouse Mom had bought me that Saturday a few weeks ago and put them on.

I took out my unopened makeup from the same shopping trip and stared at it for a long time before putting it back, still unopened.

The skirt and blouse will be enough, I decided. I've kept my part of the bargain by wearing a skirt and panty hose. Makeup wasn't in the deal.

I skipped the nail polish and the jewelry, too.

Dad whistled, and Mom said, "Wow!" when I went downstairs.

"Will I do?" I asked. "I feel funny."

"You'll do perfectly," Mom said.

"You look fantastic!" Dad said. "Are you ready to go?"

"As soon as I get my jacket," I said.

Dad carried my things out to the car. Carly, Andrea, and I were going to be arriving at Stacy's party early and staying overnight. The other guests were scheduled from eight to ten-thirty.

"You look fabulous!" Stacy said as soon as my father left. "Wonderful! I didn't think you had it in you!"

"I feel funny," I said again. "But a promise is a promise. You just remember what you're wearing to my party."

"I remember," she said. "Did you get them?"

"Right here," I answered. I unzipped my overnight bag, slid out a folder, and handed it to Stacy.

"These are great!" Stacy said, looking inside the folder. "They're going to die! Mine are great, too!" She burst out laughing, and I joined her.

I ran upstairs to drop my overnight things in Stacy's bedroom, and then hurried back down to help her set out chips and dips for the party.

We laughed again at Andrea's haul, and then again at Carly's when they arrived, though I couldn't help having a few twinges of guilt.

"Let's go set them up!" Stacy said.

Her basement was finished into one main room, a bathroom, a huge closet; and a storage room. We'd decided the storage room was the best place for our show, so we disappeared into it and set up, then finished readying the party room. Every so often, one of us would giggle.

"They'll die!" Carly said.

"We are so sneaky!" Andrea said.

"They'll hate us forever!" Stacy said.

"They deserve it," I added. "We're ready. Bring on the boys."

People started arriving, bringing presents. I was surprised how glad I was to see Mark when he came in the door with several of his friends. He smiled at me, and it was like we had a secret together, somehow.

"It was Sammy's suggestion, but it's not worms," Mark told me, grinning as he put his gift with the stack on the table. "It's a party game that says it's a lot of fun. Let's hope it is. I don't usually like party games, but Sammy said we had to play a game or it wouldn't be a real party."

When everyone had arrived and was downstairs, the first thing the boys did was sit down on the couch and the chairs, looking nervous and stiff. The girls didn't look much more comfortable standing in little groups off to the side of the room. Mark came over and stood next to me, talking, and Stacy looked surprised. I hoped she wasn't mad about Mark.

Stacy's newest interest, Christopher, was sitting with the boys. I wished I'd brought my football.

After a few minutes of nervous chatter, a few people got up and examined the food table, munching chips and vegetables.

Stacy turned on the strobe lights, and then turned on a little fog machine she had. It made a neat layer of wispy fog that slid around the floor, making the room look spooky. She turned off some of the overhead lights and started the music.

Her dad has an old reel-to-reel tape player, and he'd helped Stacy record hours of her favorite music on it so we wouldn't have to always be changing records or tapes.

When everything was arranged, Stacy stared around the room. No one was dancing. No one looked like they were going to jump up and start dancing any time soon. Except for Mark, the boys stayed on their side of the room, and the girls stayed in their little groups.

"Guys are real cowards," Mark whispered. "I know that every one of them would love to be dancing, and not one of them has the guts to be the first one out there."

"What am I going to do?" Stacy asked. "I can't force them to dance!"

"Open your presents," Mark suggested.

"I was going to do that later," Stacy said. "It always seems so greedy to open them right away."

"At least it will catch everyone's attention," I said. And maybe the game will be fun, I thought.

"Okay," Stacy agreed. She moved to the pile of presents, fiddling with them.

"Open mine first!" someone called.

"No, mine!"

The kids all crowded around, making comments and handing packages to Stacy.

"Sit!" Stacy ordered.

Everyone sat in the fog, laughing because they looked so weird with the strobe lights flashing and the fog creeping around them. Stacy looked relieved. At least people were mixing together and talking to each other.

"Good suggestion," I told Mark. "Things are loosening up already."

He grinned. "I'm a genius," he said.

Stacy opened her gifts, including one NFL T-shirt from guess who. I handed Mark his package, and he handed it to Stacy.

She thanked him, then opened it. The game was called Party Pooper, and came in a box just slightly larger than a deck of cards.

"Looks like fun," Stacy told Mark. "Thanks."

"Let's try it out," Mark suggested. "It's a party game, and this is a party."

Everyone agreed, calling to Stacy to open the

box. There was a deck of cards inside with a criss-cross design on the back and words on the other side. Stacy read the first three cards to herself and started giggling.

"We need something to spin," she said. "This is like spin the bottle. Everyone will have to sit in a circle."

Stacy found a pencil to use as the spinner, and everyone crowded around.

The pointer spun on the floor under the fog, and we had to wave our hands to whoosh the fog away to see who it had landed on.

"Bobby!" Stacy called. She shuffled the cards, picked the top one, and read, "Exchange an item of clothing with anybody else. Wear it for one dance."

"Oh, come on," Bobby protested. "That's dumb. I'm not taking off my clothes."

"Do it, Bobby," the kids called. "You could trade a sock," someone suggested. "Or a shoe."

Bobby looked around the circle. "Mark," he said, "Trade shirts with me."

"No fair," Mark said. "Yours will be too small for me!"

"You have to do it!" Stacy said. "It's your game."

"It's yours," Mark said. "I gave it to you, re-member?"

"What's the matter, are you a party pooper?" Andrea asked.

Mark unbuttoned his shirt without a word and took it off. Bobby unbuttoned his and they traded. Mark did look silly in Bobby's shirt. It was definitely too small.

"You can't trade back until you've both danced at least one dance," Stacy reminded them.

Bobby asked Andrea to dance, Christoper asked Stacy, and Mark and I started dancing, too. A few other people joined us. I silently thanked Stacy for my lessons. I was very glad I knew how to dance, even if I wasn't very good!

Mark was a good dancer and didn't seem to notice that I wasn't, so I felt more comfortable and relaxed. Stacy watched us, looking astounded, and a little angry, as Mark and I danced and talked. Actually, we were talking about football, but since the music was loud enough to cover the conversation, Stacy didn't know that.

"You look very nice," he told me.

"Thanks," I said. "I promised Stacy I'd dress up tonight. But I like myself better in my jeans and T-shirt."

He grinned at me. "I like you better in your jeans and T-shirt, too," he said. "It seems more natural."

"It is," I agreed. "And I like it better when I'm ready at a moment's notice to play football. I don't think I'm ready for a game in this outfit!"

"We'll have to get a one-on-one going," he suggested. "So I can see how good you really are.

Maybe you could join my team at the Y."

When the music ended, Stacy paused the tape player and told Bobby to spin the pencil.

This time it landed on Andrea. Stacy handed the cards to Bobby. He shuffled them, then picked one to read.

"Dance the next dance with someone who has the same zodiac sign," he read. "What's your sign, Andrea?"

"I don't know," Andrea said, giggling nervously. "My birthday's March tenth."

"You're a Pisces, then," Carly said. "Who else is Pisces?"

No one answered, until José finally said, "I am."

"May I have this dance?" Andrea asked, still looking nervous.

"Certainly," José told her. "We fish must stick together."

More people danced this time, and when the song ended, Andrea spun the pencil. It landed on Mark.

"Sing along with the next song, but sing like Donald Duck," Andrea read.

We all laughed when the next song was an instrumental. Mark complained, but finally he quacked along with the tune. Almost no one danced because we were too busy laughing, but by the time the song ended, no one looked nervous anymore.

Mark didn't spin for his turn, but no one complained. Most people were dancing by now. We didn't need the game anymore.

I walked over to Stacy. I smiled at her. "It's working," I said. "Look. Almost everyone is dancing."

"Except you and Mark," she said.

Uh-oh, I thought.

"I think you have a few things to talk over with me," she said.

"I guess I do," I admitted. "But not now. It's almost time to put our plan into action."

21.
The Plan

The party had definitely warmed up. Everybody was dancing, and the noise level had increased.

I caught Carly's eye and gave her the signal, thumb up. I nodded toward the back room. She grinned. I repeated the signal to Andrea.

I was dancing with Mark again. I was really enjoying myself, and I didn't particularly want to dance with anyone else. But I had to in order to do my part in the plan. And someone else had to dance with Mark. That was the way we'd worked it out. And even though I didn't care about the pictures very much right then, I knew the guys — including Mark — deserved what they were going to get.

"Um . . . it's no fair giving you hints," I told him. "But it's revenge time."

"Uh-oh," he said. But he was grinning.

"So just don't pay any attention to what I do, for the next few dances, okay? And don't get the wrong idea."

Mark smiled at me, and I felt that odd flutter in my stomach again. It was a strange feeling, exciting, and yet kind of scary. I actually liked a boy! Me! Jenelle!

Stacy, Andrea, Carly, and I had divided the boys who had the pictures into groups. I had Brad, José, and Gabe in my group.

Bravely, I marched up and asked Gabe to dance. He said okay.

"Great party," I said.

"Yeah."

"Kind of loud, though," I said thoughtfully.

"Yeah."

Even though the boy usually leads when you're slow dancing, I managed to angle us enough so that we were getting close to the back room. I wasn't sure how I was going to get Gabe in there. I'd considered suggesting a quiet place to talk, but he didn't seem terribly interested in talking.

Gabe noticed the door. "What's in there?" he asked.

I grinned. He'd solved the problem for me!

"Let's look," he suggested.

I opened the door and almost pushed Gabe in ahead of me.

Stacy had put two small lamps in the room, both

of them shining on a bulletin board against the far wall. There wasn't any other light.

"Hey, a bulletin board!" Gabe said. He walked right over to it. "Are these Stacy's boyfriends?" he asked.

But then he got a good look at the board. He snatched a photograph off and turned around, looking pale.

"Where did Stacy get this?" he demanded.

"Don't bother tearing it up," I said. "We have the negatives."

"Who's seen these?" he asked.

"So far, only the boys who took our package of pictures and didn't bother giving them back," I said. "Although we're thinking of conducting a tour when the party slows down. Or maybe putting up a poster in the lunchroom at school."

Gabe's mouth fell open, and he looked horrified. "But . . . I don't have any clothes on in this picture!" he said.

"I know," I told him. "I've seen it. There's another one of you up there, too. As I recall, you're using the cat's litter pan for a potty. You were sure cute at age two."

"Ooohhh!" he wailed. He turned back to the board, looking frantically at the pictures until he found the other one. He removed it, too, and stuck it in his pocket.

"Remember, we have the negatives," I told him.

"I want the negatives, too!" he said, coming toward me with his fists clenched.

"Threats won't help," I said.

"Please?" he said.

"Begging might help," I said, grinning smugly.

"Pretty please?" he asked.

"I'll trade," I said. "You get all of my pictures back to me tonight, and all of the negatives, and I'll make sure you get your pictures back. Deal?"

Dumbly he nodded. "Deal," he agreed. "But what if some of the guys didn't bring their pictures?"

"You divided them up?" I asked.

"Yes," he said. "We each took some. The ones we wanted."

"If they don't have them, they'll have to go get them," I said. "But I'll bet you brought them so you could tease us tonight. Right?"

He had the grace to look embarrassed. "Yeah," he mumbled. "You girls are really rotten, you know it? I could . . ."

"Strangle me?" I suggested.

He nodded.

"You guys took my pictures and passed them around and giggled about them in public," I said. "All we did is make a very private show in Stacy's back room. How can you call us rotten? What we did isn't half as rotten as what you did."

"Where did you get the pictures of me?" he asked.

"From your mother," I said. "We called your parents and told them what you'd done, and what we wanted to do about it. Every single one of your parents agreed you guys had it coming. They were more than happy to find the most embarrassing pictures they could and loan them to us."

Gabe growled. That's the only way I can describe the noise he made. And then he moaned.

"I'm going to burn them," he swore.

"Your mom expects the photos back tonight," I said. "She knows you've got them. You'll be in trouble if you ruin them, and besides, we can make copies. If you don't return those to your mom in one piece, we will make copies, and distribute them at school! I swear we will!"

"You girls stink," Gabe snarled.

"Don't be a spoilsport," I told him. "You deserve even worse than this. You're getting off easy. Why not be mature about this? And make sure I get my pictures back."

"You'll get them back!" Gabe promised. "I never want to see them again!"

After Gabe left I lured the other two in, one at a time. I made sure none of the other girls had someone in there, and then I got Brad, and then José in to discover the board.

Their reactions were about the same as Gabe's. They both accused me of being a rat, and I reminded them that they had been the rats first, had been the biggest rats, and had been the most public rats.

Only José was game enough to admit we'd outsmarted them, which raised my opinion of José!

I went back to dancing with Mark when I'd finished my tours.

"I've been in the back room," he said, looking half ashamed and half amused. "You girls got us good. I promised Andrea I would give you the pictures tomorrow. She said to ask you if that was okay."

"Which ones did you take?" I asked.

He looked embarrassed. "All the ones of you," he said. "Do you think I could have copies?"

"Not of the ones where I'm wearing my nightie," I said.

"Sammy wanted one of those in particular," he said.

"If Sammy asks me, I might believe that," I said.

"I'm glad you explained a little ahead of time," he said. "I wasn't too happy to see you disappearing with other boys. If you hadn't warned me to ignore it, I'd have figured you were playing a dumb game to make me jealous."

"Would you have been?" I asked.

"Probably," he said. "But mostly I'd have been mad. And disappointed. I didn't think you were like that."

"I'm not," I told him. "Although I'm not sure

138

just how I am when it comes to boys. I play football with boys, but I've never liked one before."

"Before me, you mean?"

I know I turned red because my face suddenly felt hot. I nodded. I was kind of embarrassed to admit it so plainly, but it was true. I did like Mark. I liked him in a special way that I'd never felt before.

"Then I'm your first boyfriend?" Mark asked.

I looked at him, surprised. "Are you my boyfriend?" I asked. "Just like that?"

"If that's okay with you," he said.

I smiled, surprised but pleased. "It's okay with me. As long as I don't have to give you dreamy looks and all that stuff."

"I couldn't handle dreamy looks. I'd hate it. That's why we're just right for each other. You don't act like a goofy girl, and besides, you can play football. But you play a mean trick."

"You admitted you deserved it!" I said. "I hope you guys all learned a lesson. It was Sammy's mistake to start out with. No one could have known who he meant when he said to give the pictures to his buddy. But you guys certainly knew as soon as you saw who was in the pictures! I don't blame you for looking, and even for doing a little teasing. But you were going to keep them! You went a little too far!"

"Boys tend to do that," Mark said.

A little later he and I checked the back room.

Every single picture was gone from the bulletin board. When we rejoined the party, Stacy caught my eye and grinned. She made her way through the dancing couples and handed me my photograph envelope.

"They're all here," she said. "Except for Mark's. I counted them."

"Negatives, too?" I asked.

"Yup. Everything."

"Thanks," I told her.

Mark and I danced the last two dances, and the party ended too soon.

The four of us helped people find coats, and Stacy thanked everyone for coming and for the gifts. I handed invitations to my party to the people I'd left out before. I'd decided to invite the same crowd. I'd stretched the list to include eleven boys and eleven girls, which is just exactly the right number for two teams.

And just exactly the right number for dancing.

22.
My Party

Naturally I watched the games Sunday.
But before I did, I sat Mom down and explained the change of plans in my birthday party.

"You mean, you actually want to dance?" she asked. "I don't understand. What happened?"

"I discovered it's fun," I told her. "So is it okay with you?"

"I think it sounds like fun," she agreed. "Though I'm still a little shocked. But I guess I can handle being a good sport and feeding and entertaining twenty-two people for your birthday."

"Thanks!" I told her, giving her a hug. "You're wonderful!"

"I get it from my kid," she said, hugging me back.

The boys turned out to be better sports than I thought they were going to be. Over the next week they each managed to apologize to us for keeping the pictures and for being obnoxious about them.

Stacy and I didn't get a chance to talk. She didn't call, and that kind of worried me. But I was on the phone with Mark a lot, so maybe she'd tried calling and the line was busy. She didn't act angry at school, although she did act a little funny.

Sammy gave me a bag of Halloween candy on Tuesday, explaining that he knew I didn't get to trick-or-treat much because of him. It sounded like his mom had helped him memorize a little speech.

" 'Sides, I don' like these ones," he added, snuggling closer to me.

"Oh," I said. "I have something for you, too." I'd finally remembered to pack a treat for him. I handed him two chocolate chip cookies, and he munched happily most of the way to school. Then he turned and gave me a huge, chocolately grin. He looked so adorable I had to hug him.

He slid his little arms around me, hugging back as hard as he could.

"I like you, buddy," he told me.

"I like you, too," I said, gritting my teeth. It was my fault. I should have known better. He'd hugged me so hard he'd smeared the whole front of my jacket with melted chocolate chips and cookie crumbs from his face.

* * *

I thought about Mark a lot all week. It seemed very strange to have a boyfriend! Of course, he wasn't a usual kind of boyfriend, but then, I didn't want a usual kind of boyfriend. If I'd thought about wanting a boyfriend at all, I'd have wanted a football pal that I could talk to and feel special about. And that's what I had.

He came over early on the day of my party, before the other kids arrived. He was wearing jeans and a Houston Oilers shirt, like my invitations specified. Actually, I didn't specify Oilers. I just said NFL T-shirts would be appropriate.

Mark handed me a thin, rectangular package.

"I wanted you to open it before everyone got here," he said.

"I told you not to bring a birthday present," I said.

"It's not a birthday present," he told me. "Open it."

I did, ripping off the paper in a hurry to see what my not-a-birthday present was.

It was a bracelet, with large metal links, and it said, *Mark* in scrolled letters on the nameplate.

"It's beautiful," I told him. It didn't seem like enough to say, but it was all I could think of.

"So put it on," he said. "Sammy helped me pick it out. He loves you, you know. Should I be jealous?"

I couldn't help laughing. "Maybe you should,"

I said. "I think he's adorable and sweet and I like him a lot."

"I think I can handle competition from a three-year-old," Mark decided. "Especially since he can't play football as good as I can."

The other kids started arriving. Everyone had managed to get hold of a football T-shirt, even though not all of them were NFL shirts.

We had over twenty NFL posters pinned up, each with balloons under them in team colors. Mom had ordered a football-shaped cake, and we had nuts and mints in little plastic helmets, bigger plastic helmets for chips, and tons of cans of Orange Crush.

We watched an NFL highlights show, and then it was time for our own game.

"Put your names on a piece of paper," I told everyone. "Dad's picking the teams out of a hat. He's our referee, too."

Actually, I'd arranged with Dad to cheat a little. He was going to put Mark and me on opposite teams so each team would have a decent quarterback, and he was going to divide up the kids who couldn't play football so each team got the same number.

While he was making a list of the teams, I led everyone outside and across the street for a quick warm-up.

After that we headed to the park up the street

a few blocks, carrying our basket of flags and footballs and a water jug.

"Jenelle, I thought you were my friend," Stacy hissed at me.

"What are you talking about?" I asked.

Stacy looked pointedly at the bracelet Mark had given me.

"Stacy, you said you hated him!" I said.

"I don't hate him that much!" she said, and hurried ahead to walk with Andrea.

Uh-oh, I thought glumly. But I didn't stay glum for long. Carly caught up to me next.

"Forget Stacy," she said. "She'll get over it. This is our big game, and you two are going to ruin it if you fight and grump."

"I'm sorry," I told her. "But why is she mad? She told me she hated Mark, and she was interested in Christopher now."

"I know." Carly gave me a sympathetic smile. "But you two can work it out later," she said firmly. "Now quit moping and get up and play ball!"

"Yes, Coach," I said. She's right, I told myself. This is the day she and Stacy and Andrea get to show off. They've been waiting and practicing, and it's not fair to ruin it for them. Besides, it's a party!

I joined the group, practicing and warming up. Dad read off the teams and passed out flags. Then he got out a huge roll of duct tape. He put big X's on the front and back of everyone on my team so we could tell each other apart.

I wound up with Andrea, Carly, and Jason on my team, along with Kyle and Christopher. They can all play pretty good. Then I had three girls and two boys who couldn't play, as far as I knew.

Mark had Stacy, Saul, Bobby, and José, plus five girls and one boy who couldn't play well.

So we each had six good players and five inexperienced players. I had six girls and five boys, while Mark had six boys and five girls. We were as even as we could get.

Dad explained the rules of our version of flag football. We play for one hour total, no matter how much is time out and how much is playing time. We have a three-minute break at the end of first and third quarters, and a seven-minute halftime break.

No tackling, no pushing, no yelling at the ref. Approximately seven yards for a first down, no field goals, no kicking the after-point. It's six points for a touchdown, one point for runnning the after-point in, two points for passing it in.

"All right!" Dad called. "When the whistle blows, you're on. Whenever it blows again, everybody stop immediately. Mark's team has the ball first. Line up!"

We lined up, and Dad blew the whistle. The game was on. Once we got going, I forgot about the fight with Stacy, and concentrated on the game.

Mark was good in a real game. Better than at the recess games.

But I'm pretty good, too. And we had the element of surprise! Separately, Andrea and Carly weren't as good as Mark, but they worked together so beautifully that they were almost a match for him. And because they surprised everyone with their unexpected talents, we got away with some plays we'd never have pulled off otherwise.

Unfortunately Stacy was a big surprise, too — to me! I hadn't thought about her being on the other team when I'd coached her so carefully! When she intercepted a pass I'd thrown to Andrea, I didn't know whether to cheer or complain!

The girls loved it! More than one time the guys stood with their mouths open while Stacy ran for a first down. More than once, the boys rushed Andrea and Carly, only to see them fake, fade, pass, and run like experts.

At halftime, Stacy ran over and hugged me. I almost fell over in surprise.

"I'm probably not supposed to fraternize with the other team," she said. "But I just had to tell you I'm having a marvelous time! This is great!"

"You're only saying that because you're ahead," I managed, almost too startled to tease. I wanted to ask her what had happened, but she quickly whispered, "We'll talk about it later," and ran back to her team.

They were ahead, 16–7. They'd passed for both after-points.

We pulled ahead with two touchdowns in the third quarter, but we ran in one after-point and missed the other totally, so the score was only 20–16, our favor.

We held them the whole fourth quarter until the two-minute warning. Then Jason fell while he was running for a first down, and the ball went flying loose. Stacy grabbed it and ran all the way back for a touchdown.

I just moaned. I was delighted for Stacy, but there was no way we'd catch up now. They missed their point after, but it didn't matter. Mark's team won, 22–20.

Stacy was the hero. Mark lifted her up on his shoulders and paraded around, with his whole team following after, yelling, "STA-CY! STA-CY!"

I joined them. Stacy deserved it!

"You girls were great!" Mark said. "How did you get to be so good?"

Everyone had been great sports, playing with lots of enthusiasm and making it a fun game. I felt pretty satisfied with the game, even if we had lost.

"I am starved!" Stacy called to me from her perch on Mark's shoulders. "When do we eat?"

"Let's go," I suggested, and we all headed to my house.

"Dinner's on the table," Mom said, pointing to the dining room.

I hid my grin and followed the others, almost laughing out loud at their excited comments.

"Oh, food!"

"I'm starved."

"Smells great! Can't wait!"

Then the procession came to a sudden halt, with everyone staring in shocked silence at the table. I couldn't help it. I took one look at the dog biscuits littering the table, and my old football, nestling on a bed of noodles, and I burst out laughing.

When they got over the shock of the football feast, the others joined in, laughing, too.

"I wasn't as hungry as I thought I was," Andrea said.

"Real food back in here!" Mom called.

"Actually, I'm starved!" Andrea admitted. "But let's be civilized about this. I'm sure there's enough food for all." Then she squirmed through the crowd and made it to the kitchen first.

"Grab a plate," Mom told my friends. "It's buffet style. Get your food and take it downstairs. The drinks and napkins are already down there."

She and Dad had made a Mexican fiesta with burritos, stuffed sopadillas, tostadas, and green chile to ladle over the top, with tons of shredded cheese and lettuce and chopped tomatoes.

I figured everyone would be exhausted after the game, and I guess they were — for about ten minutes. We ate in silence, chomping gratefully, and then a few people made comments about the sneak football lessons someone must have been giving.

Others started in, and pretty soon there was joking and teasing and laughter. It sounded just like a party should.

When we finished eating, we set up the reel-to-reel I'd borrowed from Stacy and started the music and the strobe lights. It wasn't very late, but it gets dark early in November, so it was dark enough for the strobe lights to be effective. With three of them on at the same time, plus light filtering down from upstairs, it was just perfect.

"No surprise pictures, I hope," Gabe whispered to me.

"Nope," I said. "A deal's a deal."

"Do I need to break out the Party Pooper game?" Mark asked me.

"No," I said thoughtfully. "With the proper example, I think everyone will figure out what they're supposed to be doing."

"I think I could be a proper example," Mark said. "Hmm. Who would dance with someone like me?"

"I would," Stacy offered.

"Oh, no you don't!" I yelped, scrambling to my feet.

"Well, somebody better claim me, or I'll feel unwanted!" Mark said.

"Oh, all right!" I told him, hiding my smile. "You guys are all alike, always wanting all the attention. I guess I could handle dancing with you at least once."

Later I cornered Stacy. "Now give," I said. "What's going on?"

Stacy looked embarrassed. "I always thought I would be the first one to grow up," she said. "Not you. And now you're more grown-up than I am."

"Wait a minute," I said. "You think I'm more grown-up because Mark gave me a bracelet with his name on it?"

Stacy nodded. "That means it's really serious," she said.

I counted to ten. Then I did it again. Finally I was calm enough to discuss things rationally. "It's not serious," I said. "It's not even like it was his I.D. bracelet. He and Sammy picked it out for me. We're not going steady or anything like that. And even if we were, that's not how you tell if someone is grown-up, and if you'd stop to think about it, you'd know that!"

"I guess I do know that," she said, after a pause. "It's just . . . I don't want you to change, Jenelle. We've been good friends for a long time, and now you're being different. Dressing up and liking boys . . . and I'm worried about whether you'll still like me."

"You're the one who made me dress up, you dummy!" I said. "I won't ever do it again, promise! And I promise not to let Mark interfere with our time together. Anytime you want to play football with me, you can."

"You really haven't changed, have you?" she said, smiling.

I never knew an evening could pass so quickly! Before I knew it Mom was calling down that the parents were starting to arrive, and I hadn't even opened my presents or cut my football cake.

Reluctantly I stopped the music, and we all headed up for cake and ice cream and presents. I got a lot of neat presents, including a lacy blouse from Stacy.

"It's my version of an NFL T-shirt," she said.

"Thanks," I told her. "But I promise not to wear it."

"You can wear it," she said, laughing. "Only not too often. I like you best in jeans and a T-shirt."

Then everyone was grabbing coats and saying thanks and heading out the door. The party was over.

And I was alone. Mom and Dad had included the clean-up as part of their birthday present to me, so they were busy downstairs.

I wandered slowly up to my room and stretched out on my bed, reliving the party. It had been a lot of fun! Football and dancing mix perfectly, I decided.

I thought about the comment Mom had made earlier. She'd mentioned that it was only four weeks ago that we'd gone shopping for "useless girl stuff."

"It makes more sense to you now, doesn't it?" she'd asked. And she was right. It did. Though I still preferred my jeans.

Yeah, I thought sleepily. A lot of things make more sense to me these days. Like Stacy. I understand her better, and I like her a lot. She's my opposite best friend. That doesn't sound right. Opposite friend? Friendly opposite?

Best friend, I decided. Definitely. And always.

I rolled over to go to sleep, planning which NFL T-shirt I would wear tomorrow. It's comforting to know that some things never change.

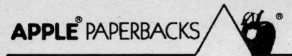